VENGEFUL HEART

THE INFINITE CITY #3

TIFFANY ROBERTS

Copyright © 2022 by Tiffany Freund and Robert Freund Jr.

All Rights Reserved. No part of this publication may be used or reproduced, distributed, or transmitted in any form by any means, including scanning, photocopying, uploading, and distribution of this book via any other electronic means without the permission of the author and is illegal, except in the case of brief quotations embodied in critical reviews and certain other noncommercial uses permitted by copyright law. For permission requests, contact the publishers at the address below.

This book was not created with AI, and we do not give permission for our work to be trained for AI.

Tiffany Roberts

authortiffanyroberts@gmail.com

This book is a work of fiction. Names, characters, places, and incidents are products of the author's imagination or are used fictitiously and are not to be construed as real. Any resemblance to actual events, locales, organizations, or people, living or dead, is entirely coincidental.

Cover Illustration by Donovan Boom

Acanthus and Samantha Art by Goku's Hairgel

 Created with Vellum

VENGEFUL HEART

When his mate is threatened, nothing burns hotter than his wrath.

Against all odds, Arcanthus found Samantha, his beautiful, sweet terran mate. His fated one. Her love shattered the barriers around his heart.

After defeating a ghost from his past, Arc thinks he and Samantha are safe to move on with their lives. But she has a past of her own, and it refuses to let her go.

He nearly lost her once. He will not take that chance again.

To all those who've suffered.
You deserve love. Settle for nothing less.

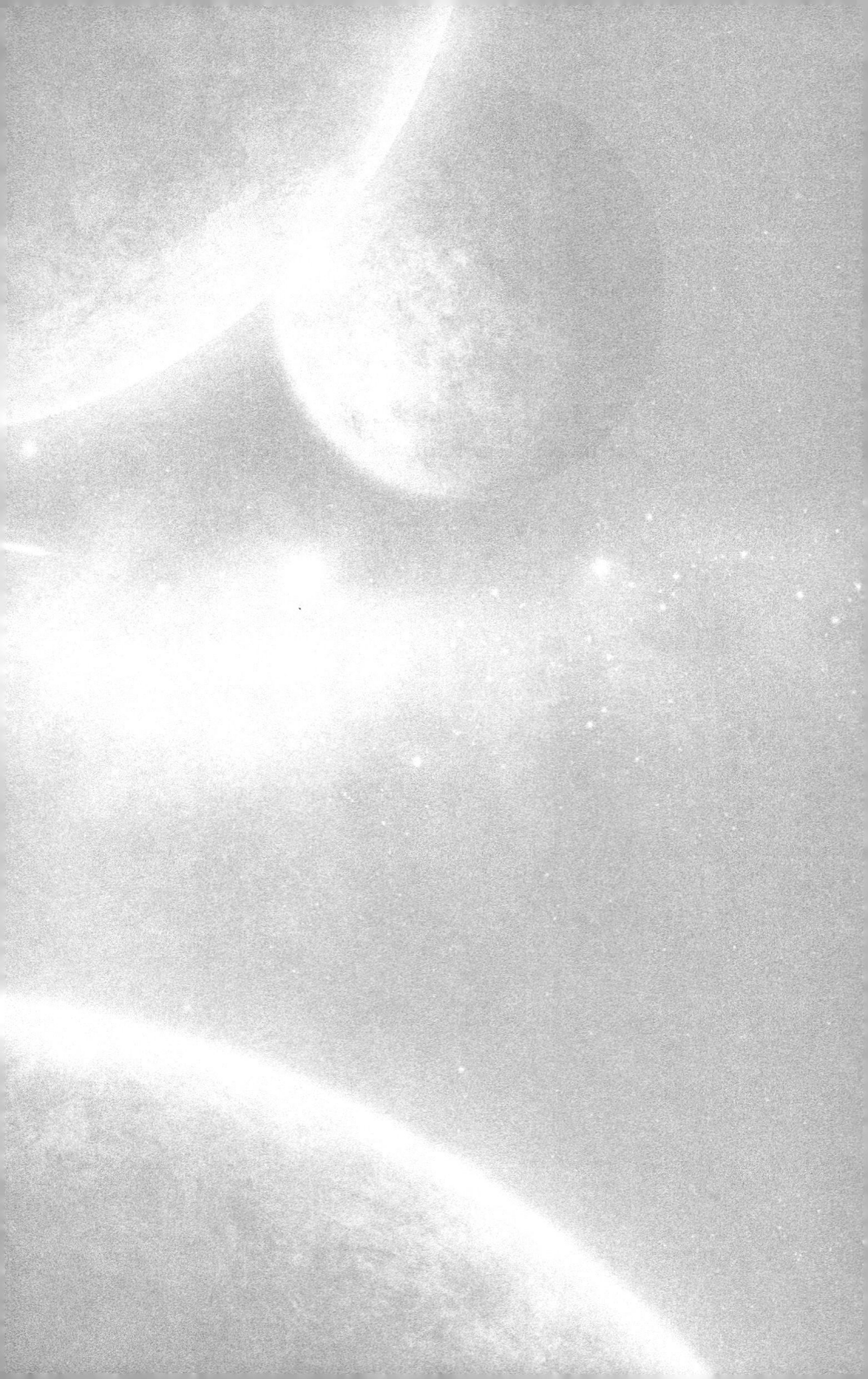

ONE

Arthos, the Infinite City
  Terran Year 2105

ARCANTHUS CLASPED his hands behind his back, settled the end of his tail on the floor, and stared out the window. On the other side of the glass, the Undercity was bustling. Hovercars sped through the air, countless pedestrians streamed along multileveled walkways and the street, shops and clubs enticed would-be customers with dazzling holograms and flashing neon lights. Yet those lights could not banish the deep, impenetrable shadows between it all.

His eyes settled on one of the many clubs below, its entrance marked by a holo of a naked dancer whose species and gender changed every few seconds.

Only meters away from that door was the spot where Arc had first touched his mate. The spot he'd first smelled her, first heard her voice, first looked into her eyes. That initial encounter had been necessitated by the callousness of the crowd, who'd knocked Samantha down and nearly trampled her to death, but Arcanthus wouldn't forget those firsts. He wouldn't allow them to be tainted.

And he wouldn't allow his mate to come to any further harm. He'd kill anyone who dared to touch her.

"*He's almost here,*" Drakkal said over the commlink.

Arcanthus tightened his grasp on his hands. Part of him wished they could feel pain, *real* pain, if only to ground him.

The soft *whoosh* of the entrance door opening broke the silence in the hotel room. Light from the corridor created a reflection on the glass in front of Arcanthus. The tall, athletic frame of a male borian was silhouetted in the doorway.

The people below continued moving, as oblivious to what was occurring in this room as they had been to the little terran who'd fallen amidst them months ago—not that any of them would've cared one way or another.

The borian didn't move from the doorway. "I think you're in the wrong room, sedhi."

His voice was calm, steady, giving away not a hint of uncertainty or surprise. A true professional, as Arcanthus had feared.

"Are you not Malthyr?" Arcanthus asked without looking back.

The borian crossed the threshold, boots coming down heavily on the carpeted floor. The door slid shut behind him, killing the reflection. "I am."

"Then it stands to reason that I am, in fact, in the correct room, doesn't it?"

"I don't recall inviting anyone in."

Arcanthus unclasped his hands and lifted one, turning his palm toward the ceiling. "I'm sure you are as tired of the endless games as I am."

Malthyr's footfalls drew closer. "You're right. So get to the fucking point."

A barely audible snicker came through the commlink, courtesy of Drakkal.

Lowering his hand, Arcanthus turned toward the borian and frowned. "Forgoing the formalities doesn't dictate a descent into rudeness, Malthyr."

The borian stood a few centimeters taller than Arcanthus and wore his black hair cropped short. His steel gray eyes were intent, wary, but his expression gave nothing else away. "Says the sedhi who broke into my hotel room."

"I didn't break anything." Arcanthus's frown deepened. "Well, unless you count the security codes, but that is a very different sort of breaking."

With impressive nonchalance, Malthyr brushed back the sides of his coat, revealing the blaster holstered on his belt, and braced his hands on his waist. "You either came here to threaten me or to sell information, sedhi. If you don't explain which one it is within the next five seconds, I'm going to blast you right through that fucking window."

Professional *and* confident.

Arcanthus's mouth curled up into a smirk. Under different circumstances, he might've come to like this brusque borian. What a shame that this meeting could only end one way.

"You're looking for a terran," Arcanthus said.

Malthyr ran his tongue along his teeth. "I asked why *you* are here. I already know what I'm doing. Talk."

"Information."

The borian's hand slid closer to his blaster. "So you don't get brief until you're told to elaborate?"

"Does it require more?" Arcanthus stepped closer; to his credit, Malthyr neither backed away nor moved his hand any closer to his weapon. Arc continued, "You're searching for a terran. Samantha Dawn Wilder. I have information regarding her whereabouts."

"My client is only willing to pay for information that leads to concrete results."

"And by all accounts, the reward for such information is handsome." Arcanthus tilted his head, and a lock of his long, black hair fell across one eye. "But I'm not interested in credits."

The borian narrowed his eyes. "And I'm not interested in negotiating."

"I have information for you, but I need information in return, and you'll happily provide it."

Malthyr's brows rose in mock surprise. "Oh? I wasn't aware you were in a position to make demands, sedhi."

Arcanthus stopped at the desk, only a few meters away from the borian, and pulled out the chair. Turning it toward Malthyr, he brushed the sides of his robe apart, baring his chest and loincloth, and sat down with his tail resting to the side. "There are a great many things of which you are not aware, my friend, and I'm afraid I don't have the time to catch you up on all of it."

That finally drew a genuine reaction from the borian—a scowl, complete with downward angled eyebrows.

Arc's smirk slanted to the side. "I'll present a series of questions. Answer to my satisfaction, and I will tell you where to find the terran."

"You have some fucking balls, sedhi."

"Yes, but they're not quite as dangly and vulnerable as yours. First question." Arcanthus raised a hand and extended one finger. "There are billions of terrans in the universe. Why this one?"

Malthyr snickered and shook his head. "I should just shoot you, but there's something fascinating about you, sedhi. You're really serious about this?"

"Oh, I'm quite serious."

The borian laughed. "All right. I'll humor you. Client wants to confirm the terran is alive and well and offer her the opportunity to return to her family."

"Something of an intergalactic welfare check," Arcanthus suggested.

Malthyr offered a humorless smile. "Something like that."

Arcanthus put up another finger. "Two. Is equipment like this"—he tugged open the desk drawer, removed a tool roll from within, and unfurled it atop the desk—"typical for such welfare checks?"

The borian's eyes rounded as they fell on the tools. His jaw muscles ticked, and his nostrils flared. "Where'd you get that?"

"Where you hid it." Arcanthus smoothed out the roll, brushing his cybernetic fingers across the items contained within. "An auto-injector, three vials of terran-made sedative, two sets of self-securing bindings, a collapsible shock baton, an ID chip jammer, and a personal sound dampener. This is all necessary to ensure a lone terran is alive and well so her family can rest easy?"

"Anything can happen in my profession," Malthyr replied through clenched teeth. "It helps to have tools on hand to deal with unexpected situations."

"Like a sedhi breaking into your hotel room."

"Yes. Like a sedhi breaking into my hotel room." Malthyr's hand crept toward the blaster.

"Third and final question." Arcanthus put up another finger. "What is the name and location of your client?"

The borian stared at Arcanthus. Slowly, his lips split in a grin, and he laughed. "Seven thunders, you *are* serious. You're really fucking serious." His laughter intensified, shaking his shoulders. "You think I'd tell you even if I knew?"

As the borian laughed, Arc wondered what Samantha was doing. He longed to be with her, to breathe in her sweet scent, and wished this situation didn't exist. Anger roiled deep within him, quiet but potent. "I'm fully aware that you don't know your client's name. I'm also aware you know far more than you're telling me."

"If you're so all-knowing, why ask me any questions at all?"

"Because I needed help deciding whether you're going to walk away from this or not."

Malthyr's laughter faded, devolving into chuckles, then a sigh, before finally falling silent. His expression reverted to its prior hardness. Behind him, the closet door slowly slid open.

"I'm going to shoot you, sedhi," Malthyr said, wrapping his fingers around the grip of his weapon, "but first you're going to give me that information you promised."

A burly, furred arm emerged from the opening closet, followed by a powerful shoulder and a broad chest. Drakkal ducked his head under the doorframe, shooting a glare at Arcanthus as he extricated himself from the cramped closet.

Arcanthus folded his arms across his chest. "I didn't promise anything. I merely set the terms for an exchange, and you've failed to uphold your side of it. You haven't answered the questions to my satisfaction."

The borian tugged the blaster free and pointed it at Arcanthus. "Where's the terran?"

"Why does your client want her?"

Drakkal moved into place behind the borian.

Malthyr glanced down at his weapon, brow furrowing. "You understand what this is, don't you? You know what it does?"

"Do you know what an azhera is? What it does?"

Drakkal growled.

The borian spun toward Drakkal, bringing his blaster up, but the azhera was faster. Drakkal caught hold of Malthyr's hand and pulled on the weapon even as he slammed the elbow of his cybernetic left arm into the small of the borian's back.

Grunting in pain, the borian staggered forward and dropped onto his knees. Drakkal tore the blaster free from the borian's grasp.

Arcanthus shoved himself up out of the chair, flicking his wrist to eject the hilt of his hardlight sword into his left hand. He activated the blade and extended his arm toward the borian, who was starting to push himself back up.

The borian's eyes widened, pupils shrinking, as the yellow hardlight blade materialized in the air before him. He froze.

The sword's tip formed a millimeter away from Malthyr's throat.

"Oh, good," Arcanthus said. "The last time I tried that, I was just a hair too close."

Drakkal adjusted his hold on the blaster and touched the end of the barrel to the back of Malthyr's head. "Didn't have a tool for this, did you?"

"No one expects an azhera in a closet," Arcanthus said.

Drakkal's eyes flicked toward him. "We're going to have words about that later, sedhi."

"I don't know the fucking client," the borian growled, his eyes filled with hate—and a glimmer of fear—as he stared up at Arcanthus.

"I believe you, Malthyr," Arcanthus replied. He shifted his hand just enough to touch the point of his sword to the borian's neck. "Now tell me... What were you actually contracted to do?"

"Find the terran. Kill any males with her and take her. Bring her to a to-be-determined meeting place to exchange her for payment."

"Well, that presents a bit of a problem, doesn't it? I for one don't want to be killed." Arcanthus looked up at Drakkal. "Do you want to be killed?"

Drakkal huffed. "Wouldn't mind wringing your neck, sedhi, but no. Not particularly in the mood to be killed."

"The fuck does that have to do with anything?" Malthyr asked.

Arcanthus frowned. "You're having trouble drawing an inference from our little exchange, are you? Don't worry. I'll explain." He leaned closer to the borian and lowered his voice. "I have Samantha Dawn Wilder. She's *mine*."

Malthyr attempted to lean back, away from the blade, but the blaster against his head prevented him from moving far. "Listen, sedhi. Listen. We can bring her in together. I'll get you the reward for the information and split my payout with you. We're talking enough credits to retire on."

"I told you, Malthyr, I'm not interested in the credits. I need information on your client."

The borian released a heavy breath through his nostrils. "I have a reputation. Discretion is important in my work, sedhi."

Arcanthus rolled his eyes, though he kept his third eye fixed on the borian. He turned his hand, shifting the sword's angle. "You understand what this is, don't you?"

"Earth. I traced the contacts I received back to Earth. They were rerouted numerous times, encrypted, but that's where it ended."

"Going to need you to be a little more specific," Drakkal grumbled.

Malthyr dropped his gaze, eyes shifting from side to side as though searching. "It was... Seattle Metro. PNW, USA. Earth. I didn't look any deeper than that."

"That mean anything to you?" Drakkal asked, glancing at Arcanthus.

But Arc couldn't immediately answer. A dreadful cold

spread through his gut, weaving through every fiber of his being, clashing with his anger and making it hotter, creating a volatile, conflicting mix that could not possibly be sustained.

His mouth was dry when he replied, "It does."

"I'll tell you anything, sedhi," the borian said. "I'm not going to throw my life away over that *ji'tas*. Anything I know, you—"

Growling, Arcanthus thrust his hand forward. The sword sank into Malthyr's throat, penetrating flesh and bone effortlessly. The borian made a soft, choked sound and reached up to weakly grasp at the blade, managing only to open deep gashes in his hands.

"Seattle," Arcanthus snarled, "is the city Samantha is from." He pulled the blade free. Blood spurted from Malthyr's throat. Arcanthus sidestepped to avoid the borian's body, which pitched face first onto the floor.

Without a second look at the corpse, Arcanthus stalked toward the door. He deactivated the hardlight sword and returned it to the compartment on his prosthesis.

"I know that look, Arcanthus," said Drakkal, "and I don't like it."

"You don't have to like it."

"*Kraasz ka'val*. You're about to do something stupid, aren't you?"

Jaw clenched, Arcanthus paused at the door, bowed his head, and drew in a deep breath. That mix of fire and ice roared through his veins, intensifying because it had no means of release. Not yet.

"Yes, Drakkal. Something very stupid, and very necessary."

TWO

Arcanthus drew in a deep breath as he woke, filling his lungs with Samantha's sweet, exotic scent. She lay with her back to his chest, her little body tucked against his. Lips curling into a smile, he nestled more securely against his mate. As much as he longed to look upon her, to see the serenity on her face as she slept, he didn't want to open his eyes, because that would mean an end to this moment.

It would mean an end to this illusion in which she was perfectly safe, in which she was free to live her life without fear, without threat.

Once he opened his eyes, he'd have to leave her to ensure that illusion became reality.

It's not like they'd ever find her. No one can hide her like I can.

His limbs—not his prostheses, but the flesh and blood limbs that had been lost to him for years—throbbed in a phantom reminder.

Just like the Syndicate would never find me, right?
Just like Vaund would never find me?

He'd nearly lost everything, everyone, because he'd believed he was untraceable. He would not make that mistake again. However tiny the chance was of Samantha being found by her ex's hunters, Arcanthus was not willing to take it.

And even if hiding her was guaranteed to keep her from harm, he wouldn't do it. It would've been the same as putting her in a cage, tossing away the key, and telling her it was for her own good. He wasn't her jailer, wasn't her master. He was her mate.

He let out a long, soft breath and opened his eyes. The bedroom was dark but for the gentle glow of the baseboard lights, which tinted everything purple. He didn't have to see a clock to know it was time.

Slowly, he lifted his head and looked down at his mate. Samantha's dark, tousled hair partially covered her face. He couldn't resist; using great care, he removed his arm from around her waist, hooked those loose strands with his fingers, and delicately brushed them back. Her features were relaxed in sleep. If she harbored any worries, doubts, or fears, they had no effect upon her now.

Until she could exhibit the same relaxation during her waking hours, he would not stop fighting for her.

Arcanthus let his gaze roam over her face, emblazoning every detail on his soul, just as he had so many times before and would do again and again for the rest of his life. For all the words he knew, he had none that were adequate to describe how beautiful she was in his eyes.

His gaze dipped, following her neck to the pale flesh of her shoulder.

He swept his eyes down her body, and his smile widened. She was covered from the chest down but for one dainty foot poking out—a foot that would undoubtedly be colder than the lightless void of space were she to touch it to his skin.

And he would welcome that touch. He'd welcome any touch from her, whether it was fiery or icy, tender or rough, soothing or arousing.

Desire quickened within Arc, urging him to run his palm over her skin, to draw away the blanket and reveal her delicious body to his ravenous gaze. Heat curled in his belly, swiftly followed by an ache in his cock. He clenched his jaw.

Since their first joining, Arcanthus had partaken of Samantha's body every day without fail, often more than once. His hunger for her was insatiable. The thought of being away from her for days, perhaps even weeks... It made him want her all the more right here, right now.

His cock pressed through his slit, its tip splitting. The tendrils brushed across the smooth, soft skin of her ass. Every muscle in Arcanthus's body tensed, and his breath caught in his lungs.

Now. It has to be now.

If he didn't leave right away, he wasn't sure he could bring himself to leave at all. He wouldn't have that shadow hanging over her head, whether she was aware of it or not. He couldn't do that to his mate.

She had suffered enough. He would do all in his power to prevent her from spending even another moment in fear or pain, and if that meant shedding blood, he'd do so without hesitation. Any threat to her would be dealt with swiftly and mercilessly.

Arcanthus released his breath slowly through his nostrils and shifted his hips back, breaking the contact between his cock and her tantalizing skin. Then, with the utmost care, he propped his torso up and extracted his cybernetic arm from beneath her pillow.

Samantha stirred. Drawing in a deep breath, she turned her head toward him, lashes fluttering open. "Arc?"

His chest constricted, making his heart skip a beat. Hadn't it been hard enough to leave already? He whispered, "Go back to sleep, Samantha."

With a throaty hum, she shifted onto her back and stretched her arms over her head. The blanket slid down with her movements, uncovering her lush breasts. Sighing, she settled, and her eyes closed once more.

Everything in Arcanthus stilled as he stared down at his mate.

Fuuuuuck.

He clamped a hand over his groin. His cock pressed hard against his palm, its tendrils writhing with need.

Shouldn't have lingered. Should've just forced myself out of bed...

Keeping that hand firmly in place, he rolled away from her and sat up. Every motion only intensified the ache beneath his palm. Lifting his legs—each of which ended just above the knee—he scooted toward the edge of the bed using his free hand and his tail.

How could he ensure the threat to Samantha was eliminated if he couldn't even bring himself to leave the bed? If he couldn't get himself to venture beyond arm's reach, he certainly wasn't going to manage crossing the known universe.

The quicker I depart, the quicker I can return to her.

Finally, he reached the edge, where he'd set his prosthetic legs last night. As he pulled the protective coverings onto the ends of his legs, fitting them around the cybernetic sockets, he was hit by the realization that he could no longer recall how it had been with his real limbs intact. He couldn't remember how they'd looked, couldn't remember the scars and imperfections, the lines on his palms or the length of his claws.

And none of that mattered because he had Samantha.

Even without his cybernetic limbs, Samantha saw him as perfect.

Bracing his hands on the bed, he drew himself forward and dropped his thighs into the fittings on his prostheses. When their sockets reached the internal connectors, they clicked into place. Sensation buzzed through his body as the cybernetics interfaced with his nervous system.

The soft brush of fingers along his back sent enticing, more powerful sparks across his skin, forcing him to suck in a breath.

"Are you leaving now?" Samantha asked, voice husky from sleep.

His reply caught in his throat, and he battled to get it out, to say that single word that was so much heavier, so much harder, than it had any right to be. "Yes."

There was a rustle of cloth, and Arcanthus fought the urge to look back at his mate. But then she was there, her warm body pressing against his back and her long hair tickling his skin as she looped her arms around his neck to embrace him.

She touched her forehead to his temple, just beneath his horn. "I'll miss you."

Arcanthus grasped her forearm, squeezing gently. "It won't be long, Samantha."

But it would feel like forever. Whether it was weeks or days, their time apart would feel like an eternity.

She kissed his cheek. "I know. But I will still miss you."

He turned his head toward Samantha and brushed his lips against hers. His desire flared, flooding his veins with heat. He hated fate for putting her in danger and forcing him away from her.

More than anything, he hated the person responsible for this situation.

"I will miss you too, my flower," he said when he withdrew his lips. "So much so that it already hurts."

She met his gaze. Her brown eyes were so big, so alluring, so full of love, longing, and concern. "Couldn't you just...stay?"

He smoothed his palm over her cheek as he brushed tousled strands of her hair back. "I yearn for nothing more. But there is a final matter from the past to lay to rest, one more ghost to banish. And it is something I must do in person. I'll not have anyone else handle this in my stead."

"I understand."

She turned her face and kissed his palm. He felt only the echoes of it through his sensors. Loosening her arms, she pulled away, taking all the warmth with her.

"Were you... Were you really going to leave without saying goodbye?" she asked quietly.

Her words were like a blade piercing his heart. No physical blow could have pained him more than the hurt he'd caused her in that moment.

What had he hoped to accomplish by slipping off while she slept? Had he been trying to avoid the heartache of saying goodbye, of having to see the sorrow in her eyes? Had he been trying to spare Samantha...or himself?

It didn't matter. It didn't matter what his reasons had been, because nothing could have justified it. He shouldn't have tried to depart that way, and he'd been a damned fool for thinking it had been the right thing. If he and Samantha were to be apart, if they were to be countless light years away from each other, even for a little while, he would not let *this* be her last memory of their time together.

Arcanthus turned toward his mate. She sat on her heels with her hands on her thighs, her breasts bared, and her long hair hanging loose around her. The purple light bathing her skin was quickly replaced by the golden glow of his brightening *qal*. Her wounded eyes met his.

He needed her. Needed to feel her. He needed her to feel

him, needed to imprint himself upon her very soul again and again. Needed her to know that he lived and breathed for her.

A growl rumbled in his chest; the sound vibrated through him, rousing a primal force deep inside that strengthened his need beyond reason.

Arcanthus flattened his hands atop the bed and leapt at her.

Samantha gasped and fell onto her back. Arcanthus landed over her, catching himself on hands and knees. She stared up at him with wide eyes. Her hands lay to either side of her head, and those pert breasts rose and fell with her rapid breaths. Alluring heat radiated from her skin.

Slipping his fingers into her hair, he cradled the back of her head and tipped her face up toward him. "I was a fool to think I could leave without saying goodbye to you." He lowered his face and kissed her, nipping her lower lip with his fangs before pulling away. His tongue slipped out to soothe the spot. "Without tasting you."

He curled his tail and ran it up her inner thigh, stroking it across her sex. The tip pressed on her clit, making her breath hitch and her lashes flutter. Arcanthus grinned. "Without seeing you come undone with pleasure."

He lowered more of his weight atop her, absorbing her heat, delighting in her softness. With his voice becoming low and husky, he whispered into her ear, "Without making love to you."

Settling her hands on his shoulders, she caught her bottom lip with her teeth and let out a muffled moan as she undulated her pelvis against his tail. A tremor to swept through her. "Arc..."

Supporting himself with one hand, he reached back, grasped her thigh, and guided it around his waist. She lifted her other leg on her own.

"I was a fool to think I could leave without reminding you, Samantha"—he withdrew his tail and wedged himself between her thighs, his throbbing shaft sliding along her slick folds—"that you are *mine*."

"I'm yours," she whispered.

He took one of her hands off his shoulder, pressing it onto the bed and lacing their fingers as he captured her mouth in another kiss. Though his yearning had not diminished, he let that kiss linger, drew it out, caressing and teasing Samantha's lips and tongue to coax soft sounds of want from her. The tips of his cock's tendrils stroked the sensitive flesh of her mons, desperate and hungry to be inside her wet heat.

She bucked her hips against him, making him shudder with a jolt of pleasure. Arcanthus growled and pushed his pelvis forward, keeping his shaft trapped against her, denying her the fullness she sought—denying himself at the same time. Samantha whimpered.

"First, my flower, I'll drink my fill of your nectar." He shifted his body down, kissing her neck and chest, her nipples, her belly. "Though it will not be enough to prevent the maddening thirst I will endure without you."

Arcanthus released her hand as he moved lower, running his palms over her shoulders, across her breasts, and down her sides. By the time his mouth was positioned over the glistening petals of her sex, she was panting softly. He drew in a deep breath. Her heady aroma clouded his mind with a delectable lust haze.

Curling his fingers around her inner thighs, he spread Samantha's legs wide, pushing them flat to the bed. "My beautiful, sweet, sweet mate."

He dragged the flat of his tongue from the bottom of her sex to the top, gathering her slick, and twirled the tip around her clit. She gasped, thighs tensing beneath his palms.

An appreciative growl rumbled from Arc as her taste danced across his tongue. His cock, pinned between his pelvis and the bed, twitched and pulsed, nearly making him shudder anew. He withdrew his tongue only long enough to snarl her name before lapping greedily at her flesh, flicking and teasing the little bud that brought her so much pleasure.

Samantha moaned and grasped his horns, holding his head in place as she undulated against his mouth. "More."

Arcanthus looked up along her body and met her gaze. Her half-lidded eyes gleamed in the dim light, and her shallow breaths came through parted lips. His tail lashed behind him. Those splashes of pink on her cheeks never failed to excite him. He pressed his pelvis down, rubbing his shaft against the bed, and speared her pussy with his tongue.

"Arc!" Samantha cried, tilting her head back.

He thrust his tongue in and out of his mate, drinking the delicious nectar that flowed from her core. His fingers tightened on her thighs, pinning them in place even though she made no attempt to escape. Something within him—something instinctual, something bestial—demanded he lay claim to her, demanded he conquer her.

"Please, oh God, please, Arc," she begged, writhing against him. "I need you now."

He thrilled in these moments, when Samantha's inhibitions disappeared to reveal the sensual, passionate being she truly was beneath her shy and quiet exterior.

Her thighs quivered, her breaths quickened, and her inner walls contracted. Withdrawing his tongue, Arcanthus clamped his lips around her clit and sucked.

A hitched, broken sound escaped Samantha, and her back arched off the bed. It was swiftly followed by her cry of pleasure.

As her body convulsed in the throes of ecstasy, Arcanthus

lifted his head and pulled his horns free from her grip. He shoved his body up and over her, braced himself on one elbow, and stole her cries with an uncompromising kiss.

Reaching between their bodies, he grasped the base of his cock and forced the tendrils together, pressing their tips to the entrance of her sex. Maddening heat radiated from her in waves. With a fierce snap of his hips, he thrust into her.

His groan mixed with her moan as she wrapped her legs and arms around him and clutched at him. Her sex pulsed with her continued orgasm. Each wave of her pleasure echoed through him, assailing him with sensation he could barely resist. She was so wet, so hot, so tight, so fucking perfect.

"I love you," she whispered against his mouth, smoothing her hands up his back to delve into his hair.

Arcanthus cradled her jaw in his hand and looked into her eyes. "You are my universe."

He reclaimed her lips, demanding everything from her—and promising everything in return. She responded with equal fervor.

He pumped his hips, maintaining the contact between their mouths despite the shockwaves of pleasure blasting through him with each slide of his shaft. Every thrust was more powerful, more urgent than the last, sending him deeper and deeper, and she welcomed him. Her body drew him in, ravenous for more.

All that sensation couldn't stop his thoughts from running wild, and the questions that arose sped his already racing heart.

What if he hadn't found the borian bounty hunter before Samantha had been located, what if he had failed to discover the threat? What if he had lost her? A trip to the local market could've meant disaster, a simple walk outside could've been the end.

What if she had been taken from him?

Those led to the heaviest question of all, the one that made his insides twist and sink, that made his throat tighten and his heart stutter.

What if he'd never found Samantha to begin with?

Such thoughts didn't normally plague him, but here and now, on the cusp of leaving her alone for the first time since she'd come to live with him, he could not stop them. And all that fear, all that uncertainty, only served to heighten his need for her. It only served to strengthen his instincts.

She was his. She had to know it, had to feel it. She was his forever.

And he was hers.

Growling, he tore his mouth away from Samantha's and pushed himself up. Keeping one hand on the bed, arm straight, he dropped the other to her waist and took hold as he drove into her faster, harder, each pump of his hips punctuated by a snarl. His fingers curled; if he'd still had his natural hands, his claws would've pressed into her flesh, adding pricks of pain to her pleasure.

"Mine." He reared back onto his knees and moved his other hand to her waist, lifting her backside off the bed and using both arms to slam her against his pelvis over and over.

"Always," Samantha rasped. One of her hands caught her breast, squeezing it, while the other gripped his knee. "I'll always be yours."

His pace grew savage, unforgiving, relentless, and he grunted through bared teeth as fire blazed in his veins. Pleasure coiled within him, winding tighter and tighter. Every thrust inside her brought him closer to euphoria.

Mine.

The word repeated in his mind each time he slammed into her.

Mine. Mine. Mine!

She was all, she was everything, she was his purpose; she was the source of his pleasure, his joy, his comfort. Nothing mattered but Samantha. Nothing existed but Samantha.

Her heels dug into his backside, and her inner walls clamped around his cock, drawing him impossibly deeper, as she sucked in a harsh breath. She trembled, mouth opening wide in a soundless cry.

"Mine," he growled again, keeping his hips moving. "All mine."

Samantha's hands darted to his, grasping and clawing at his prostheses. Her back arched, and her body went taut, caught on the edge. Sensation thrummed along his shaft, into his groin, and raced along his nerves, leaving his entire being abuzz with pleasure. But he needed more. More of her.

"Give me everything, my flower, my mate. Give me"—he drove into her hard, burying himself to the hilt—"*all*."

Her voice rose in raw, ragged ecstasy, and a rush of liquid heat surged from her core. Arc's roar joined her cry as his pleasure burst past its peak. His muscles seized, and the tendrils of his cock flared open, latching onto the inside of his mate to pour his hot seed into her. This time, he held *nothing* back. He gave her exactly what he'd asked of her—everything.

Gritting his teeth, Arcanthus fell over his mate, gathering her in his arms as he and Samantha were engulfed by rapture and rode out the sensual waves of bliss. She cradled him against her body. Again and again his seed flowed into her, filling her womb, and for a moment, he hoped.

He wanted it to take.

As the spasms in his cock grew weaker and further apart, Arcanthus's awareness returned to the present. His breath was ragged, his heart thunderous, and Samantha was smoothing her hands up and down his back while trailing soft, tender kisses on his shoulders and neck, following his *qal*. His skin tingled delightfully beneath her ministrations.

He looked down at her, meeting her gaze. Her eyes were still half-lidded, now bright with satisfaction, and the smile on her lips was soft. Her skin glittered with perspiration in the gentle glow of his *qal*.

She reached up and swept aside the stray strands of his hair, tucking them behind his ear. Her smile faded. "Promise you'll come back to me. Promise me you won't get hurt."

"I swear I will come back to you, Samantha," he replied, stroking a thumb over her cheek and curling his tail around her leg. "Nothing will keep me from you."

She tipped her face up and pressed her lips to his. He leaned into the kiss, savoring its sweetness, its tenderness, and the yearning still underscoring it. If their lovemaking had been fueled by the fiery, explosive passion at their cores, this kiss was the quiet affection and adoration they shared the rest of the time, the enduring connection that made every moment they shared precious.

He remained like that, embracing her, until his cock finally released its hold, and he was able to withdraw from her sex. But even then, he couldn't bring himself to leave. She curled up against him, sheltered in his arms, and he stroked her hair soothingly, relishing her closeness, her warmth, her scent.

Their scent.

This was what he would hold on to while he was away—this moment, this intimacy. He would uphold his promise even if it meant battling from one side of the universe to the other just to return to this.

To return to *her*.

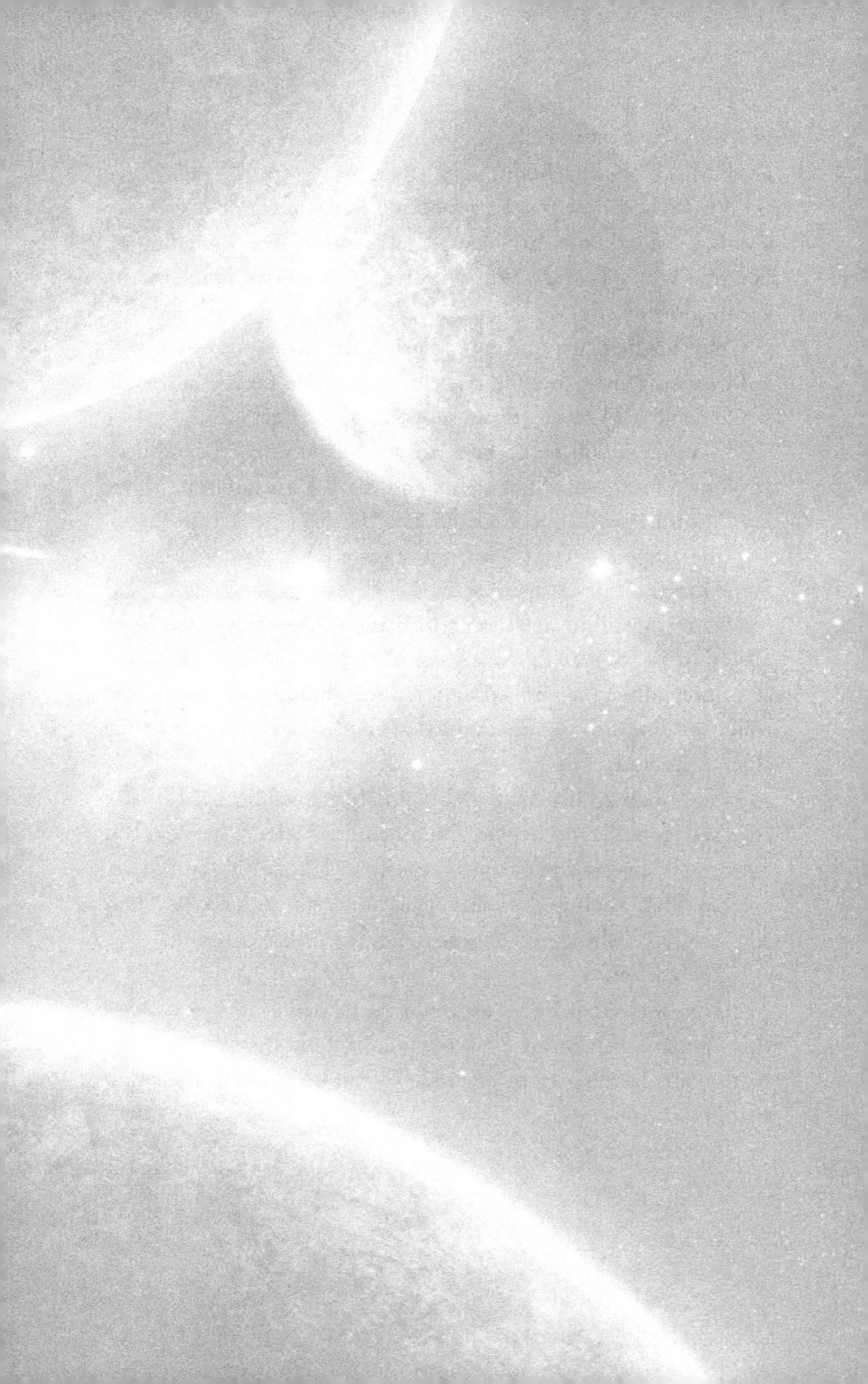

THREE

Arcanthus tipped his head back, taking in the view before him. Only days before, he'd been standing in front of a very different window, looking out upon a very different sight, with his emotions just as mixed as they were now.

When he'd first seen the holographic images of Samantha in the Consortium's database, he'd been immediately enraptured. But those holos had not done her justice. They could never have compared to her in the flesh. The same could be said of Earth—he'd seen it in dozens of holos, but nothing compared to seeing it like this, dominating the view though the space station window.

The expansive blue oceans, the brown and tan deserts, the varied greens of plains and forests, the patches of white cloud; the view was stunning.

This was where Samantha had been born. This was where she'd grown up, where she'd lived. Where she'd experienced so much joy and pain before she and Arcanthus had ever known of each other's existence. Looking at his mate's home world like this was...humbling. It was a glimpse of her he'd never thought he would have.

And it felt wrong that she wasn't here. He longed to have her at his side, to have her in his arms, to share this moment with her. He longed to see this world through her eyes—because he knew, despite the hardships she'd faced here, his Samantha would still recognize the beauty on display.

"These terrans are lucky," said Urgand.

Arcanthus glanced at the brown-skinned vorgal. "Why do you say that?"

Urgand scratched his cheek, where his tattoo—vorgal symbols in the rough shape of a shield gathered around a war hammer—marked his status as a former Vanguard, and adjusted the strap of the travel bag slung over his shoulder. "The first species who contacted them were friendly. A lot of people out there would've seen a planet like this and wanted to conquer it for themselves. And the terrans wouldn't have stood a chance."

"What a grim way to say you admire the view."

Sekk'thi chuckled. The female ilthurii stood on Arcanthus's other side, head tilted as she stared out the window, her tail slowly swaying behind her. "He was forged in war. That is how he sees many things."

"Yeah," Urgand agreed. "Guess it doesn't always make for the most pleasant conversation."

"No need to worry," Arcanthus replied. "We all I know I keep you around for your good looks, not your conversation."

"You're probably fucking with me, sedhi, but I'll take it as a compliment."

"I'm completely serious, vorgal."

Sekk'thi looked past Arcanthus, her violet eyes raking over Urgand from top to bottom. Her scaled brows shifted up before she faced forward again. "Earth is beautiful. Just like Sam has said. And there is so much water... I wonder what the beaches are like."

Urgand grunted. "Probably a lot like most places where an ocean hits the land."

The ilthurii's lips twitched down; the slight frown was about as expressive as her scaled face could be, but Arcanthus glimpsed a wistful glimmer in her eyes.

"I suppose it falls upon me to remind you that we are here for business." Arcanthus stepped back from the window and gestured down the corridor. "And we really should get to it before we miss our shuttle."

Urgand laughed and slapped Arcanthus on the shoulder. "You're the one who stopped to admire the view, not us."

"I would have regardless," said Sekk'thi.

"We're here to curb his impulses, not reinforce them."

Arcanthus started walking. "You're here because a certain someone refused to let me travel alone."

His companions fell into step behind him.

"Doesn't contradict what I said, does it?" Urgand asked.

Laughing, Arcanthus shook his head. Urgand and Sekk'thi's presence was another part of this trip that left him conflicted. He was grateful for their support, and he knew he could rely on them—especially for the sort of work that lay ahead. This business was likely to involve a degree of subtlety that a few members of the team would've struggled to achieve, whether due to their imposing size, like Razi, or their demeanor, like Thargen. The cren brothers, Kiloq and Koroq, were exceptionally observant and patient, making them perfect for defending the compound.

And Drakkal was the only one Arcanthus trusted to safeguard Samantha in his absence. That left Sekk'thi and Urgand the natural choices for this journey. The ilthurii was easygoing, adaptable, and practical. The vorgal was a veteran combat medic, and he had always been calm and collected even in emergency situations.

But after everything that had happened with the Syndicate, Arcanthus wasn't happy about involving his friends in something that could endanger them. This wasn't about them, wasn't their problem to solve, yet they'd been eager to help.

Everyone loved Samantha. It was still difficult for Arcanthus to keep in mind that their love for his mate was *friendship*, and that he had no reason to be jealous.

As they made their way to the planet-bound shuttles, Arc tried to pretend that the crowds of terrans weren't strange. There were more humans here than he'd ever seen or could ever have imagined. But no matter how many terrans he saw, one thing would always remain true.

Samantha was one of a kind.

They found the private, self-piloting shuttle Arc had reserved, stowed their bags, and boarded, with Urgand and Sekk'thi sitting beside each other. Arcanthus input their destination. Once the vehicle departed, he activated his holocom and engaged a jammer that would block all recordings inside the cab.

"We good?" Urgand asked.

Arcanthus nodded.

"What's our plan going into this, then?"

Leaning his head against the cab wall, Arcanthus looked through the holo viewport and shrugged.

"We have a target, right?" Urgand continued. "A location, a source of weaponry, a way to avoid local authorities?"

"No."

Sekk'thi leaned back in her chair, her long tail curling around in front of her legs. "No to which?"

"Most of them?" Arcanthus replied.

Fire sparked across the viewport as the shuttle entered Earth's atmosphere.

That feeling deep in Arcanthus's gut intensified. The days-long journey to Earth had been surreal. Part of him hadn't been able to believe he was traversing the universe, that he'd left the Infinite City for the first time in a decade. But reality asserted itself as fire blazed around this little shuttle and Arcanthus crossed into an alien atmosphere.

"Arcanthus..." Urgand growled.

"What do we have?" asked Sekk'thi. The dancing light from the flames made the emerald scales of her headcrest glimmer.

"We have a hunch," Arc said.

Urgand's brows fell. "You said you knew who was behind this. That you knew who sent the bounty hunter after Sam."

Arcanthus frowned. "I know exactly who did it, Urgand. I don't happen to have any concrete evidence of it, but I *know*."

"We came halfway across the fucking universe on a hunch? Are you... I don't..." The vorgal's nostrils flared with a heavy exhalation, and he shook his head. "No wonder Drakkal was against this. Klagar's Balls."

"Arcanthus would not take a journey like this without being sure," Sekk'thi said. She turned her head to glance out the viewport at the land far, far below.

"Thank you, Sekk'thi. That's why I brought you along. I know you trust me." Arcanthus punctuated those words with a glare at Urgand.

The vorgal stared back blankly. "Strange. Thought you said we were only here because Drakkal forced you to bring us."

"I brought *you* because Drakkal forced me. I brought Sekk'thi because I enjoy her company."

The ilthurii laughed, and Urgand muttered a curse, but

even he smiled after a few moments; the expression softened when he glanced at her.

Arcanthus eyed the pair briefly before returning his attention to the viewport. Tightness spread through his chest, complementing the sinking weight in his gut. "I've spent a long time hiding. A long time hoping the past wouldn't catch up to me, believing that I was doing enough to ensure it wouldn't. But I was wrong. And I'm not going to remain idle while my mate is in danger. I'm not going to pretend that hiding in a fortress of my own creation is enough, because it never was and never will be.

"No more waiting. He came for my mate, and now I will end him. He doesn't get another chance to attack. He doesn't get a single fucking breath more than what I allow him."

"Fuck," Urgand rasped. "You know how to get a vorgal excited, I'll give you that. But it'd still be great if you actually had some kind of plan."

Sighing, Arcanthus dragged a hand down his face. "To put you at ease, Urgand, I will say that there is a plan. It's simply... too malleable for me to share the details at present."

"That doesn't put me at ease. Not at all."

"Do not worry," Sekk'thi said, patting the vorgal's thigh. "You are skilled at fixing things, especially amidst chaos. All will be well."

"I think you're overestimating my skills. I'm just the one that keeps people from bleeding out long enough to get to the person who does the actual fixing."

"Perhaps that is what you were." The ilthurii bared her teeth in her version of a smile. "I was once meant to be food, but that is not what I am now."

Urgand chuckled, and his blue eyes dipped, looking her over. "I don't know, Sekk'thi... I think I'd still take a bite."

She tilted her head; though her smile didn't change, the

new angle of her face added mischievousness to the expression. "Whenever you would like to try, vorgal, you are welcome. But this food will bite back."

Arcanthus sat back, looking from the vorgal to the ilthurii and back again. "The worst part about this situation is that I find myself unable to comment about this blatant flirtation, lest I be crushed beneath the weight of my hypocrisy."

Urgand's eyes widened, and he looked away from Sekk'thi quickly, making a sound that was half cough, half growl. "Not flirting."

Sekk'thi watched him from the corner of her eye. "Vorgals do not flirt. They simply take what they want. Is that not the way of your kind, Urgand?"

The vorgal raised an arm to scratch the back of his neck. "Uh...yeah. That's right."

The side of Arcanthus's mouth quirked upward. He wished this were a recreational trip, one to be enjoyed by himself, his mate, and his friends. They'd certainly earned it, especially after their deadly battle with Syndicate forces.

"Anyway, Arc"—Urgand cleared his throat—"you never said who you think is behind this."

Arcanthus shifted his gaze to the viewport. The flames were gone now, leaving an unobstructed view of the clouds and the land below them. The answer formed in his throat, but the words were thick and heavy, bristling with anger and hatred. He forced them out anyway.

"A rather wealthy terran from a city called Seattle."

"Guess that makes sense. It's not cheap to abduct someone from Arthos and bring them back here."

"Especially someone with a Consortium chip," Sekk'thi said.

Urgand frowned, and a crease formed between his brows.

"Why go after her, though? There's a whole fucking world full of terrans right here."

"Because there is no one, terran or otherwise, like Samantha," Arcanthus replied more harshly than he'd meant to. He couldn't dull that edge as he continued. "And this wealthy terran happens to be her former betrothed."

FOUR

Arcanthus emerged from the master bedroom to find Sekk'thi sitting at the table, staring at the New York City skyline through the large windows, and Urgand sitting on the couch, drinking water from a rather expensive looking bottle. The vorgal's eyes shifted to Arcanthus.

Urgand choked and sputtered. Water sprayed from the sides of his mouth and poured down his chest to soak his shirt. He pulled the bottle away, dripping more liquid, and coughed, face darkening.

Sekk'thi turned on her chair and grasped its back as though she were about to get up, her eyes rounded.

"He's fine," Arcanthus said, folding his arms across his chest. "Earth water is just a bit much for him to handle." He watched as the vorgal, still coughing, bent over and wiped his arm across his mouth.

"What the fuck, sedhi?" Urgand finally rasped.

Arcanthus blinked, keeping his third eye slightly out of sync with the other two.

Pressing his lips together to muffle a fresh bout of coughing,

Urgand lifted his free hand and gestured to Arcanthus from top to bottom.

Frowning, Arcanthus spread his arms and glanced down at himself. He'd changed into a suit tailored in a volturian-inspired style—modified, of course, to account for his tail. The dark fabric accentuated his physique. He smoothed down the front of his jacket; as the material shifted, it shimmered with subtle patterns.

"Not the reaction I'd hoped for," Arcanthus said. "You may well have ruined my entire evening, Urgand."

"Whatever, sedhi. Seriously, what are you wearing? Magama's flailing teats, you don't look anything like yourself right now."

Sekk'thi tilted her head and looked over Arcanthus. "I think it looks good."

"Proving once again that you are my favorite." Arcanthus waved toward Sekk'thi. "Be more like her and you might earn yourself a raise one day."

Urgand snorted and pushed himself up off the couch. "Everyone knows Drakkal handles the payroll. You'd probably shit yourself if you knew how many raises he's given me over the years."

As the vorgal walked into the suite's kitchenette, Sekk'thi turned her chair toward Arcanthus. "Is there a reason for this new clothing? It is very different from what you usually wear."

"That's exactly the point." Arcanthus strode to the window. This place, this New York City, reminded him of the Undercity—the signs and lights, the traffic, both vehicular and pedestrian, the towering structures climbing up into darkness. Of course, New York had a few more terrans around, and there was an actual sky to look at. "My preferred clothing tends to draw attention when I'm out and about. This is to help me blend in."

"I'm sorry, boss, but I don't think it matters what you wear," Urgand said as he grabbed a towel from one of the drawers. "You're not the sort who's capable of blending in."

"Well, neither are you."

Urgand shrugged before scrubbing the towel over his face and neck. "Never claimed to be. But there are a fuck of a lot more vorgals on Earth than sedhis."

Sekk'thi bared her sharp teeth in a smile. "You are both correct. But why do you need to blend in while we are in this room?"

"And you didn't even try very hard. You don't match the upholstery at all," Urgand said with a laugh.

"This may come as a surprise to both of you, but we *will* need to leave the hotel to conduct our business here on Earth. You know"—Arcanthus lifted a hand, fingers directed down, and swung two of them alternatingly—"walk outside."

The vorgal frowned. "So you didn't bring us here to relax in a luxury suite?"

"We have been misled," Sekk'thi sighed dramatically.

"To think we trusted you, boss."

Arcanthus braced a hand on his hip and shook his head. "And here I thought I brought along the serious members of my security staff. Perhaps I should've just come with Razi."

"You know exactly what he'd be doing," the vorgal replied.

"I also know exactly what he wouldn't be doing—insulting his employer."

"Admit it, Arc. You like the attention."

"You can shut up now, Urgand."

Sekk'thi slid her chair away from the table and stood up. "Do we need to change clothing?"

"What for?" Arcanthus asked.

Urgand wadded the towel and tossed it onto the counter. "We're heading out and getting to work, right?"

"We?" Arcanthus glanced down at himself again and grinned before returning his gaze to his companions. "Oh, I see. My apologies for any confusion. We will all have to leave the hotel at some point, but tonight *I* am leaving. Alone."

The vorgal's expression darkened.

"Don't glare at me like that, Urgand."

"You really think you're going out alone?" Urgand asked.

"No. I know I'm going out alone."

"I want you to use your imagination, boss. Put everything you can into it. Picture yourself standing here with Drakkal and telling him what you just told us, and then tell me what his response is."

"*Kraasz ka'val*, Arcanthus," Sekk'thi said in a low, exaggerated growl, "did you suffer a blow to the head?"

Arcanthus snorted in a failed attempt to stifle his laughter. "You've certainly captured his essence, Sekk'thi, but the accent could use a little work."

Though Urgand had also laughed, his humor faded swiftly. "We're going with you."

"You're not, but I appreciate your thoughtfulness." Arcanthus strode toward the door, tail swinging leisurely behind him. "I'm going to meet an old friend who might be able to help."

"An old..." Urgand huffed, braced his hands atop the counter, and leaned toward Arcanthus. "Why didn't you mention anything sooner about having a contact on Earth?"

"Didn't I mention it during the trip?"

"No," Urgand and Sekk'thi replied in unison.

Recoiling slightly, Arcanthus shifted his gaze between the two. "Well, you know now, anyway."

Eyes rounded and lips parted with something akin to disbelief, Urgand shook his head. "How the fuck have you stayed alive for so long?"

"Sheer stubbornness." Arcanthus reached for the door control.

"We're coming," the vorgal growled.

"Did you not hear the bit about me being stubborn?"

"This isn't a joke, sedhi."

With a sigh, Arcanthus turned to face his companions. "This friend is...moody. All three of us showing up unannounced isn't going to make him happy."

"So let him know we are coming," Sekk'thi suggested.

"That's not going to work. Our dynamic is"—Arcanthus waved a hand as he searched for the word—"unique."

"So we'll wait outside," said Urgand.

"*Or* you could wait right here." Arcanthus pointed at the floor with both hands. "Sound good? Excellent."

"Arcanthus..." Urgand warned.

"No, no. There's a plan in place now, vorgal, just like you wanted." Arcanthus reached back with his tail and hit the button, opening the door. "You can't deviate from it now."

With a bitter chuckle, Urgand hung his head. "Drak's going to fucking kill us."

Arcanthus grinned, spun around, and stepped through the doorway. Just before he closed the door, he heard Sekk'thi say, "Drakkal will only find out if Arc actually does get himself killed."

The vorgal's curse in response was audible even through the sealed and sound-dampened door.

FIVE

I am fine, Arcanthus typed. *Urgand is overexaggerating.* He tapped the send icon.

The response came swiftly. KRAASZ KA'VAL, YOU FUCKING RAN OFF ALONE ON AN ALIEN PLANET! IN WHAT REALITY IS THAT FINE?

This one, obviously, Arcanthus replied.

He dismissed the holocom screen and lowered his arm, looking through the hovercar's side window to watch blurred streaks of color passing outside the hyperway tunnel.

He had to give the humans credit—this was a fascinating transportation system. The publicly available information he'd found about it described the hyperway as a jump drive in a tube, and that seemed about right. The tunnels allowed hover vehicles to travel at speeds immensely faster than they could otherwise have achieved, effectively connecting the entirety of Earth.

According to the information, anyone could hop into their hovercar, enter the hyperway, and travel anywhere in the world within a few hours. All Earth-made hover vehicles interfaced with the hyperway's systems to automatically guide themselves to their programmed destination.

Another message alert sounded from Arcanthus's holocom. He glanced at the dashboard display; according to the autopilot, the vehicle was four minutes away from its destination.

Four minutes was plenty of time for Drakkal to send a torrent of messages. When the azhera got going...

"Fuck." Arcanthus sighed, lifting his arm again to unlock his holocom.

To his surprise, the new message wasn't from Drakkal, but from Samantha. His heart sped, pouring warmth into his veins that annihilated his irritation. He opened the message.

Hey! Sorry it took me so long to reply. I was showering when you sent your message, so I didn't hear the alert. I'm so glad you made it safe. Can't say I wasn't worried sick over here. I can't wait until you get back. Also...you stole my sparring partner!

Arcanthus smiled despite the tightness in his chest. He'd never known it was possible to love someone as much as he loved Samantha, and he'd never known it was possible to miss someone so much that it physically hurt. He continued reading.

Everything has been good here. Everyone's trying to keep me occupied, and Drak is playing Mama Bear. Or Mama Kitty, I guess. He's also mad at you. You should see the way his fur is standing on end right now.

But nothing's the same without you here. I know you're busy, but... If you have time, maybe we could have a holo call soon? I really want to hear your voice and see your face. I miss you.

Love you. Stay safe.

"Ah, my little terran..." He closed his eyes and pictured her face. As much as he yearned to feel her skin against his, to feel her body tight around his shaft, to hear her cries of pleasure, it would've been enough in that moment just to have her close so he could look into her eyes and see her love shining out.

This was the longest he'd ever been apart from his mate. Regardless of all the distance he'd traveled over the last few days, regardless of all that remained to be done, he was tempted to board a ship and return to Samantha with all possible haste. Nothing mattered but her.

Which is why I'm here.

No threat to Samantha would be tolerated. For her, Arc would find a way to unravel time, to move galaxies, to do anything it took to keep her safe and let her know that she was loved more deeply and fiercely than anyone in all existence.

Arcanthus opened his eyes and typed out a response, his frown deepening with every word.

I miss you more than I can express, my flower. I wish I was there with you. I trust that you'll keep everyone in line, Mama Kitty included. As much as I want to call, I'm going into a meeting in a few minutes. But we will connect soon. I promise.

I love you.

"And those three little words don't even come close to telling you how much," he rasped.

He forced himself to send the message before he could add anything more. He could've sat there and written for hours and hours, could've poured his heart into text, could've happily chatted with Samantha until the cosmos finally unraveled, but he wouldn't allow himself to do so. Not while this shadow loomed over her.

And for now, it was best that she didn't know of the plot against her, that she didn't know what Arc meant to do to stop it. When the time was right, he would he tell her what he'd done, and he would beg her forgiveness for keeping the secret.

But he would never doubt that this was the right thing to do.

The hovercar guided itself to the side of the tunnel, seamlessly joining a stream of vehicles flowing into an exit tube. The streaks of color outside the hyperway slowed and dulled; ahead, a wide exit gate loomed, rippling with energy.

Arcanthus sat up and swung his legs down.

Soon, Samantha. I'll be with you again soon.

The hovercar passed through the gate. Arcanthus squinted against the sudden brightness, but his eyes rapidly adjusted to what lay before him.

If New York had been reminiscent of the Undercity with its verticality and efficient use of space, this place much more resembled Arthos's surface. Los Angeles sprawled out before him, stretching as far as he could see to the north and south. There were tall buildings all over, but nothing like he'd seen in the New York skyline—there was so much open air here, so much light. The sun had been setting in New York, already leaving deep shadows in the streets, but here it was high and bright.

And again, he couldn't help but wish his mate was here with him to appreciate the view.

The vehicle banked north, flowing with traffic into a high-speed lane. After another two minutes, the hovercar began its descent, finally landing in a residential neighborhood comprised primarily of apartment complexes.

With a few quick commands, Arc's holocom located and interfaced with the local security and surveillance systems, all of which were operated by the city government. He picked out all the recorders within range and hacked them, fixing their cycles in a temporary loop.

As far as anyone was concerned, after all, he was never here.

Arcanthus exited the vehicle. Raising his arms over his head and extending his tail, he arched his back and stretched with a grunt. The forty-five-minute journey from coast to coast had felt tenfold as long because he'd only had his thoughts—and Drakkal's fury—to occupy him.

He lowered his arms, straightened his clothing, and strode to the apartment complex. The security gate leading into the courtyard had a callbox set beside it listing residents and their apartment numbers. He found the one he was looking for—312—and pressed the button.

The soft droning of hover vehicles speeding through the air far overhead drifted down to him. Somewhere else, high, wailing sirens echoed through the streets. Much closer, animals chirped songlike calls and children laughed and shouted as they played. All those sounds were familiar and yet foreign, just different enough on Earth to be oddly intriguing.

After a brief scan of his surroundings, he pressed the button again.

Seconds passed. Arcanthus sighed and muttered, "I come all this way, and they don't even have the courtesy to be home precisely when I have need of them?"

With another glance around, he directed his left hand at the gate and performed the gesture to engage his holocom's lockbreaker program. Not half a second later, the locking mechanism clicked.

"Oh no, someone left it unlocked." Arcanthus pushed the gate open and entered the courtyard.

The apartments were arranged around the inside of the courtyard in five levels, which were connected by several staircases. A swimming pool with clear water lay at the center, and the planters arranged around the space contained tall trees with wide, long leaves at their tops.

He took the first set of stairs up to the third floor, rounded the walkway, and stopped in the entrance alcove to apartment

312. He tapped his knuckles against the door and turned his head to listen.

There was no answer.

Well, I certainly hope this is the correct address.

Directing his hand toward the door latch, he repeated the lockbreaker gesture. The sounds of distant hovercars continued, slightly amplified in the breezeway, and the bassline of loud music rumbled from one of the nearby apartments, but there was no immediate click.

Arcanthus released a huff through his nostrils. He tapped a finger against his thigh, fighting the urge to let his eyes wander; that would only make him seem suspicious, and as his companions had so helpfully pointed out, he wasn't exactly inconspicuous to begin with.

The latch clicked. Arcanthus grasped the handle and slowly opened the door, keeping his body well behind his leading arm. Fortunately, no alarms went off, no weapons fired, and nothing exploded as he entered the apartment. He closed the door behind him, relocked it, and glanced around.

The place was modestly furnished and decorated, comprised of a small living area with an adjoined kitchen and a few doors, two of which were open. One led into a bedroom, the other into a lavatory. The colors were muted—grays and blues, primarily. There were a few pictures on display, some of them holos, some of them old-fashioned printings, and a stylized sculpture of a female dancing stood beside the couch.

The place was somehow both nothing like he'd imagined and exactly as he'd expected.

He wandered about briefly, examining the living room with care; considering who lived here, he very much doubted the residence was as mundane or innocuous as it seemed. But he hadn't come to ransack someone else's home and examine their personal belongings.

Arcanthus sat on the couch, brought up his holocom, and connected it to the holographic entertainment system before leaning back with one arm stretched along the backrest. A holographic screen projected from the wall. He bent a leg, settling his ankle across the opposite knee, and slowly scrolled through the various entertainment, sports, and news channels. After a decade in the Infinite City, it was strange to be presented with so much that he didn't quite recognize or understand.

He'd chosen something familiar—a melodrama starring a mixed volturian and terran cast—when the front door latch clicked again.

With a flick of his hand, Arcanthus turned off the holo, and then quickly arranged himself in a reclined position with both arms draped over the back of the couch.

The door swung open. A female stepped into the apartment, awkwardly carrying two large bags. Her face was downturned as she presented her back to the room, kicked the door closed, and awkwardly locked it.

Turning, the female stepped into the room, glanced up, and halted. The bags dropped to the floor with a crash. Her right hand dipped with unexpected speed and swept aside the fabric of her long shirt. It snapped back up clutching a small blaster pistol, which she aimed at Arcanthus.

He smiled wide. "Hello, Abella."

She blinked, and her jaw dropped. Slowly, she brought left wrist, where she wore her holocom, to her mouth. "Perform search. Can pregnancy cause hallucinations?"

Arcanthus chuckled. As the holocom replied with information about hormonal changes and their effects on the human mind, he looked her over. It had been nearly a year since he'd seen Abella Mitchell, and she'd certainly changed. Her black hair was shorter than he recalled, and it was no longer dyed blue at the ends. Her skin had a healthier glow, her green eyes were brighter—and she was quite clearly with child. Abella still had those long, lithe limbs, but her belly was rounded, and her breasts were fuller.

He'd been so intrigued by her back then. So much so that it had prompted him to search for a terran of his own. If it were not for her and Tenthil asking for his help, Arcanthus might never have found his Samantha.

A sudden longing struck him. He wanted to see Samantha's belly swelling with their child. He wanted to press a hand over her belly and know there was a new life growing inside—a life that they had created together.

Fuck. He'd entertained those thoughts from time to time since he and his mate had first spoken about it, but this craving was on a far deeper level.

He forced those thoughts back, though they did not go easily. This wasn't the time to dwell upon such matters; there'd be time to dream after his business on Earth was done. He waited for Abella's holocom to fall silent before speaking.

"I am not a hallucination, terran. I'm flesh and blood." Brows falling low, he waved a hand. "And metal, I suppose."

"Oh. Okay... So I'm not going crazy." Her blaster remained steady as she adjusted to a two-handed grip and narrowed her eyes. "What the fuck are you doing in my apartment, Alkorin?"

"Visiting old friends."

"Friends don't usually break in when they come to visit."

Arcanthus tilted his head and grinned. "Well, I'm not the usual sort of person, am I?"

"No, you're not. I never thought I'd see you again." She wrinkled her nose as her gaze moved over him. "What are you wearing?"

"Why does everyone take issue with my clothing?" He spread his arms. "I happen to be the sort of person who looks amazing in *anything* I wear, and even better when I don't wear anything at all."

Abella snorted. "That doesn't suit you at all." She tilted her head and frowned. "Why are you here, anyway? We paid you more than your asking rate."

"You don't need to keep your weapon pointed at me. At the risk of sounding audacious, please"—he patted the couch cushion beside himself—"sit and talk with me."

Abella arched a brow. "Sit and talk? You came all this way just to...talk?"

"You and your mate once sought my help. Now I'm coming to you."

She lowered the blaster and frowned. "You need our help?"

"Well, *his* help, but I wouldn't dream of excluding you."

She rolled her eyes and snorted, but finally holstered the blaster. "Just so you know, Tenthil doesn't do that kind of work anymore." Carefully crouching with one hand supporting her rounded belly, she reached for the food items that had spilled from the bags.

Arcanthus pushed himself off the couch, walked to Abella, and offered her a hand. "I caused this mess. I'll clean it for you."

Abella pointed a finger at his face. "I'm still not interested. I'm *very* happily mated"—she turned her hand and wiggled a her fingers, one of which glittered with a ring—"and married."

"And with child. Congratulations," Arcanthus said, taking hold of her hand. He helped her rise. "I am also very happily mated. As for married..."

She narrowed her gaze. "What is that look? What does that mean?"

"Perhaps I do need your help after all, Abella."

SIX

With a swipe of his thumb, Tenthil deactivated the hoverbike's atmospheric shielding. Wind swept in around him, ruffling his hair and making his jacket billow. He breathed it in deep.

Countless scents mingled in his nose, not all of which were pleasant. Though Abella had told him that the air quality here had greatly improved over the last several decades, it still bore hints of smog and industrial pollution, enhanced by the ozone tang of electronics running in the sun. Concrete and metal rounded out those scents. But there was so much more than that—the fragrance of varied plants, the rich smell of the Earth itself, the aroma of hundreds of different foods cooking and dozens of different species coexisting.

Strangely enough, that blend of scents had come to represent freedom for Tenthil. This was the air he'd breathed as he and his mate had begun building their lives together. This was the air he'd breathed as they were married, as they'd watched Abella's belly grow with their child, as they'd dreamed out loud about the home they desired, a home beneath open skies, a home with trees and grass and room for their child to run and play.

He guided the hoverbike down, and his burgeoning excitement intensified. This was the best part of every day—when he came home to her. His mate. His Abella.

His contract with the United Terran Federation had him training terran soldiers at military bases out in the desert and, sometimes, in orbit. Despite being six months into the contract, he'd not yet grown comfortable around the soldiers.

At their core, they weren't that different from the Infinite City's Eternal Guard. They represented authority, order, law; everything Tenthil had been trained to avoid and evade. His role had been to stalk, strike, and kill, efficiently and mercilessly, before vanishing into the shadows. Even if he no longer performed that work, he'd been unable to shed all that the Master had ingrained in him.

Spending his days in hot, cramped spaces with soldiers who triggered instincts that had been beaten into him throughout his life was more draining than he could have imagined. He wasn't supposed to be training governmental forces. They were an enemy. Perhaps *the* enemy.

It was fortunate that his status as a contractor left him outside the military hierarchy. After his experiences in the Order of the Void, he never wanted to submit to anyone's authority again. He would make his own way for himself, his mate, and their youngling.

And yet the officers who served as his liaisons seemed pleased with his work, and they'd mentioned that his training was already making a difference. He and Abella had seen the news story circulating only weeks ago—a covert team of UTF specialists had located and rescued ten humans who'd been recently abducted by slavers.

There'd been no additional information provided about the military team, but he'd known. Tenthil had trained them.

And that...felt good. Apart from Abella and her family, he had no connection to this world or its people, and yet he could not hear about terrans being abducted without thinking of her, without remembering the state she'd been in when he'd rescued her from Cullion's manor. Without recalling the electrolash marks, the bruises, the too-pale skin, the alarming amount of weight she'd lost in a matter of days.

Tenthil had been taken as a child and had suffered for most of his life, but that suffering had forged his strength. If he could use that strength to spare others such pain...wasn't that a worthwhile cause? Wasn't that the perfect way to spit on the Master's legacy and rise above it?

The antigrav engines thrummed between his legs as he brought the bike down atop the parking garage. He pulled into his designated spot, killed the engine, and paused to wipe a speck of dust off the instrument panel.

All that truly mattered was his mate. Abella was his reason for being here, his reason for striving to improve himself, to claim a happy, peaceful life. She was his reason for accepting the UTF contract and doing this work.

And she was the reason it was so, so hard to leave every morning.

His every instinct demanded he stay with her, protect her, cherish her, and those instincts had heightened exponentially since the start of her pregnancy. When he woke beside Abella each day, she called to him—her body, her scent, her soul. And he rarely resisted.

They'd taken to referring to it as their morning exercise...or, sometimes, their first breakfast.

A grin curled on his lips.

Tenthil dismounted the hoverbike and strode toward the

stairs, sped by sudden ravenousness. He wanted his mate. Now. Needed her, now.

But even that desire couldn't stop him from scanning the vehicles parked in the garage as he passed them, couldn't stop him from studying the people he saw. A few of the hovercars were unfamiliar, but the faces were not.

As he descended the open-air staircase, the park shared by the surrounding apartment complexes came into view. Children of several species played on the colorful equipment and ran through the green grass, laughing and talking and shouting.

Tenthil had seen many strange things since coming to Earth, but this was amongst the strangest—and the most heartwarming. Children in the Order learned to be silent and serious. There was no play, only training.

But before that...there was play. There was joy. With my people, under moon and stars...

Not for the first time, he imagined himself and Abella down there with their child, running in the grass, laughing, tumbling and rolling, climbing and swinging, and he smiled to himself.

All those things you took from me, I am finding again. One by one. Your shadow is withering in the sun, Master.

When he reached the third-floor landing, he crossed to the apartment complex's breezeway. His eyes continued roving, as they always did; Arthos was behind them, and the Master was dead, but Tenthil would never cease his vigilance.

In some ways, he was more on edge living in a place like this. Life seemed too peaceful, too quiet. There were rarely issues in this area. That didn't seem natural, not after spending most of his life in Arthos's underworld.

None of the people he saw outside were strangers; even if he hadn't spoken to most of them, he knew their names, knew the apartments in which they resided. No strangers present. No reason for alarm.

The Order died with the Master.

Hadn't it?

As he neared the entrance to his apartment, a scent struck him that made his steps falter. A drop of venom flowed from his fangs, its sting jolting his tongue. He gritted his teeth. He knew that smell. It was distinct, unforgettable...

But he'd only ever smelled it in the Infinite City. Only ever smelled it in Nyssa Vye, when he and Abella had gone to see—

No. It can't be.

The smell was only stronger when he reached the door. Masculine, spicy, exotic.

A growl rumbled in Tenthil's chest. He checked over his shoulder to ensure no one was in sight, flexed his fingers to extend his claws, and drew his tristeel knife from his belt. Well aware that the lock made an audible click whenever it disengaged, Tenthil unlocked the door and shoved it open, bursting through with energy crackling through his muscles. The door banged against the wall hard enough to bounce, slamming itself shut just behind him.

He barely noticed.

Little he'd encountered in his life had surprised him enough to stop him in his tracks, but what he saw now halted Tenthil's advance utterly. Shock, confusion, and raw, fiery rage swirled in his chest, and he bared his fangs with another growl.

A sedhi was lounging on Tenthil's couch, only meters away from Abella, who sat on a nearby recliner chair. Though the sedhi was dressed in a dark, tailored suit, his leisurely, sprawling posture and yellow-on-black eyes were unmistakable —as was that arrogant fucking smirk.

"Ah, Tenthil," said Alkorin the Forger, "so lovely of you to join us."

Abella smiled sheepishly and gestured toward the sedhi. "We, uh, have a guest."

Tenthil charged across the room. Leaping from her chair, Abella placed herself in his path, throwing her arms wide. His heart stuttered. Using every muscle in his body, he stopped himself an instant before he would've crashed into his pregnant mate.

She didn't move, didn't so much as flinch; she just kept her eyes on him. "Tenthil, don't."

Behind her, Alkorin remained in the same relaxed position, his expression unchanged but for a slight widening of his smirk.

"Move," Tenthil commanded, his glare fixed on the sedhi.

"Not until you put that knife away and promise you're not going to hurt him," Abella said.

"He won't feel pain for long."

Alkorin chuckled. "And I had been led to believe you don't kill people anymore."

Tenthil leaned toward the sedhi, baring his fangs. "Willing to make an exception."

Abella rolled her eyes and placed her palms on his abdomen. Slowly, she smoothed them up his chest, over his shoulders and neck, until she cupped his jaw. At her urging, he turned his face toward her.

"You're not going to kill him," she said.

When his mate looked at him with those big green eyes, with that gentle yet stern expression, when she touched him so soothingly with those soft but confident hands... No one could calm his soul, no one could ease his violent instincts, like she could.

"He's dangerous," Tenthil rasped.

"He helped us."

"He wanted to rut you."

Abella chuckled. "He was respectful about it." She glanced over her shoulder at Alkorin. "Mostly, anyway."

Tenthil snarled and drew back, shaking off his mate's hands. He was going to kill the sedhi. And then when Alkorin was dead, he'd find a way to kill him again just to be sure.

"I'm kidding! I'm kidding!" Abella wrapped her arms around Tenthil and lay her head on his chest. "I'm sorry. Probably not the best timing for a joke."

"And at any rate, I would never describe what I do as *rutting*," Alkorin said. "There's far more skill and artistry at play."

Again, Tenthil pushed toward him. "You fu—"

The sedhi threw up his hands, displaying his metal palms. "I'm not here for your mate, zenturi. While I can admit that I might have obsessed over her for a bit longer than was healthy in the aftermath of our dealings, I've since found my true mate. I've no desire for anyone but my Samantha."

"You have a mate," Tenthil said flatly. "*You*."

Alkorin's smirk vanished, and a hard light entered his eyes. "And I would not betray her for anything."

"He has a terran mate." Abella tipped her head back to look at Tenthil. "She's why Alk is here." She reached up and stroked his jaw. "He came to ask for your help."

Jaw muscles ticking, Tenthil glanced from his mate to Alkorin. "I refuse. Leave."

Abella frowned. "Tenthil."

"We only just escaped everything he represents, Abella. I will not let him drag you and our child back into it."

"Alkorin helped us when we needed it most. He is the reason we were able to start over, the reason we're here right now, in this apartment that we've made our home. The reason we're able to live in peace."

Tenthil's fingers tightened around the grip of his knife.

With his free hand, he cradled the back of Abella's head. "We paid him for that. Business, not charity. That was what he said."

She scowled and drew back an arm to poke his chest.

"Arcanthus," the sedhi said.

Tenthil gritted his teeth. "That supposed to mean something?"

"It's my name. My real name. I told you Alkorin was one of many aliases."

"That supposed to sway me?" Tenthil met the sedhi's gaze.

Arcanthus shrugged. "I meant it as an extension of trust, but you may interpret it as you will."

Abella slid her palm along Tenthil's arm until it came to rest over his fist, which was still closed around the knife. "Please, Tenthil. He's not here to hurt us. He just needs your help."

"My mate is in danger," Arcanthus said. "I will do anything to keep her safe. Hence the casting aside of my pride and my presence here. I will gladly pay you for any services rendered, zenturi."

Tenthil returned his attention to Abella. He couldn't help but think of the danger she'd been in, couldn't help but recall the things he'd done to protect her. He'd gone to war with the order of assassins that had shaped him. He'd torn down everything he'd known—and he would have ripped the whole universe to pieces, had it been necessary.

Taking firmer hold of Abella's hair, he leaned down and breathed her in. Her scent was even more alluring than it had been when he'd first met her. Her eyes remained locked with his.

With a low growl, he slanted his mouth over hers, claiming her lips with a savage kiss. And she opened to him, responding eagerly. She slipped her fingers into his hair, her body growing pliant against him, as she flicked her tongue over the points of his teeth.

Sweet venom trickled from his fangs, and his cock hardened. His instincts demanded that he claim his mate now, that he assert dominance over this would-be rival, that he prove himself the stronger male.

Those instincts would not be denied.

Something kicked against his abdomen, startling Tenthil to awareness.

Abella chuckled, breaking the kiss and opening her eyes to grin at him. "She's reminding us that we have company."

Perhaps his instincts *could* be denied. For a short while, at least.

"Please, do not allow me to interrupt," said Arcanthus.

"Can I at least hurt him a little?" Tenthil asked, the words emerging from his burning, damaged throat in a rough whisper.

Abella pressed another kiss to his lips. "No."

Releasing a heavy breath through his nose, Tenthil returned his knife to its sheath. He placed a hand over his mate's belly and shifted the other to the side of her neck, cupping her jaw. Their daughter, who was due any day now, pressed against his palm. Abella's pulse thumped steady beneath his fingertips. His mate, his child, his family...his everything.

If Arcanthus's mate was in danger, just as Abella had been back in Arthos, how could Tenthil deny him aid? He understood the sedhi's fear, his desperation. Understood it all too well.

He didn't look away from Abella as he said, "Fine, sedhi. But I will not kill for you."

"I'm not asking you to kill anyone, zenturi," Arcanthus replied. "I just need your help getting to him."

SEVEN

The hallway was eerily quiet as Arcanthus walked to his suite. Any noise here was devoured by the cushioned, patterned carpet and the sound dampeners undoubtedly installed everywhere, allowing the hotel's guests to rest without having to hear their neighbors.

Arcanthus didn't care for it. Silence itself didn't bother him, but the silence in this place triggered some instinct that urged him to move as quietly as possible so as not to break it. He wasn't a recruit trying to sneak back into the barracks after a long night out, or a youngling attempting to evade his parents' notice after breaking curfew. He was a grown male who was accountable only to himself.

Well, myself and my mate. But she's not here.

And damn if he didn't wish she was.

Why did it feel like he was doing something wrong?

I am in the process of breaking several UTF and intergalactic laws with the intent of breaking at least a few more, but that has nothing to do with what I'm feeling right now.

With a low growl, he increased his pace and tugged at the

collar of his shirt. It was the suit that was bothering him. It was restrictive, suffocating, wrong. It felt like a lie.

I've used almost two dozen aliases over the last ten years, but this is too much for me?

"I suppose I must acknowledge the possibility that being away from my mate is slowly driving me to madness," he muttered. "All the more reason to be done with all this swiftly."

Finally, he reached the suite, opened the door, and stepped inside. The windows looking out at the skyline had been blacked out, and all the lights were off but for a faint one in the kitchen, which only deepened the shadows in the rest of the suite.

The door quietly closed behind him, and Arcanthus padded forward.

A dark form stirred on the couch, releasing a heavy breath. Voice made thick by sleep, Urgand asked, "Boss?"

"Yes," Arcanthus replied as he walked past the couch and entered the kitchen. "And as your boss, I feel I must point out that groggily calling out to a potential intruder in the dark of night doesn't seem like a particularly effective means of maintaining security."

Urgand snorted. "You gave us the night off."

Arcanthus opened the refrigerator. "I don't recall saying that."

"Well, that's how I remembered it, and you weren't around to argue."

"Fair enough." Bending down, Arcanthus perused the contents of the fridge. The food cartons in the front meant Urgand and Sekk'thi must've ordered dinner earlier. He opened one of the containers.

"Stay out of our leftovers," the vorgal grumbled.

"I was just looking."

"It's rude."

Arcanthus scowled and resealed the container. "So is not getting me anything."

"That's what fucking happens when you leave without saying where you're going or when you'll be back."

"I can't argue that," Arcanthus said with a sigh. He checked through the various beverages that had been provided by the hotel; only the water was familiar. He settled on a bottle of orange liquid which was, unhelpfully, labeled as *orange juice*. Clumps of pulp had separated and settled on the bottom of the container.

"A color is not an ingredient." As he shook the bottle, he closed the fridge, walked to a nearby cabinet, and retrieved a drinking glass. "Why are you sleeping on the couch, anyway? Did you fall asleep trying to wait up for me?"

Urgand sat up and tilted his head to the side, cracking his neck. "Easier to monitor threats from out here."

Arcanthus opened the container and poured the juice into the glass. "Isn't that benefit nullified if you're asleep?"

"I'm a light sleeper." The vorgal stood up and walked toward the table near the darkened windows. He was wearing only a pair of undershorts, and the dim light couldn't hide the scars on his body from Arcanthus's keen eyes. None were quite as bad as Thargen's, but they illustrated a life of conflict, of battles hard-fought and not always won.

"An acquired trait?" Arcanthus closed the juice container and returned it to the refrigerator.

"Picked it up in the Vanguard." Urgand paused at the table and braced a hand upon it. "If the medics weren't constantly on alert, people died. More people, I mean."

Picking up his glass, Arcanthus exited the kitchen and went to join the vorgal at the table. "For what it's worth, Urgand, I am honored to have you on the team. Even more so to count you as a friend."

"I see how it is. Sneaking in late after running off and then trying to soften me up with sweet talk." Urgand glanced at Arcanthus and grinned. "Still pissed at you, sedhi."

Arcanthus dragged his tongue across his teeth. "I'm being sincere here."

Urgand chuckled. "I know, Arc. You dress it up in twenty layers of fancy shit and deflective humor, but you can't hide your core."

With a cybernetic hand, Arcanthus gestured down at himself. "There isn't much left of me beyond my core."

"There it is." The vorgal laughed, but that laughter was cut short by a yawn. "Fuck. How late is it, anyway?"

"It's not late."

Narrowing his eyes, Urgand picked something up from the table and pointed it at the window. The black tint faded, restoring the glass's transparency.

Dawn light shone between the towering buildings, flooding the hotel room and banishing the illusion of night. Urgand turned his face toward Arcanthus and folded his arms across his chest.

"What? I didn't lie." Arcanthus nodded toward the window. "It's early."

"You're impossible, sedhi."

Arcanthus lifted the drinking glass to his lips and sipped. Humming in surprise and delight, he held the drink up to the light. "Who would've thought orange is so delicious? And I'm not impossible, Urgand. Just improbable."

Urgand's lips parted with a slow, heavy exhalation, and he stared as Arc took another sip of the sweet, tangy juice. Arcanthus fixed his lower eyes on the skyline but kept his third eye directed at the vorgal. He drank his orange juice and watched the sunlight intensify, watched the air traffic thicken, watched droves of pedestrians bustle along the streets.

"If I do not wither beneath Drakkal's glares, do you think yours will do any better?" he asked.

"You wouldn't say anything if it didn't bother you."

One of the bedroom doors opened.

Arcanthus shifted his third eye forward and drained the rest of his juice, sighing in satisfaction when it was done. "According to all of you, the only time I'll ever be silent is when I'm dead."

"Talk of death is no way to greet the sunrise," Sekk'thi said as she walked over to the males.

"Even if death is our business?"

Urgand grunted. "Today the day?"

Placing the glass on the table, Arcanthus stepped to the window and tapped a knuckle upon it. He'd spent so much time looking out at the world through holo screens or panes of glass, foolishly believing he was safe because he'd kept himself apart.

But fate always found a way in.

Even within his secure compound, he'd often locked himself away from his friends, from the people he trusted and adored. He'd hidden himself from everything. But that had changed. *He* had changed. Because of Samantha. She'd given him reason to leave his isolated, controlled environment. She'd reminded him that living and surviving were two different things—and that the latter did not necessarily lead to the former.

My, my. Aren't I just full of deep, dark thoughts this morning?

"No, today is not the day," Arcanthus finally replied.

"Can you give us something here?" Urgand asked, dragging his fingers through his hair. "Anything?"

"My contact is looking into it. If they can't find a way, no one can."

"What're we talking?"

"Not sure yet." Arcanthus glanced over his shoulder. "Tight security, most likely, but nothing that would be out of place in the Gilded Sector. The wealthy on Earth are just as protective of their privacy as the wealthy back home. The public records of his address end at the house he shared with Samantha, but he's moved somewhere else, and he's kept it hidden. Even if our target only recently inherited his fortune, he's already taking full advantage of it."

Sekk'thi lifted Arc's empty glass and sniffed it, making thoughtful hum. She swished the last few drops around the bottom. "Is it really the same everywhere? The same sorts of people holding the wealth and power?"

Clenching his jaw, Arcanthus looked ahead again, shifting his gaze higher. Clouds that were still partially shadowed drifted across the brightening sky—a sky beneath which he should have been standing with Samantha. "I don't know, Sekk'thi. But I'd like to hope not."

"We'll leave our mark, regardless," Urgand growled. "Might be tiny, and might never get noticed by most people, but we'll fucking leave it. For Sam and everyone else who's suffered. For...you, Sekk'thi."

Arcanthus turned around to face his companions. The vorgal and ilthurii stood with their gazes locked. Her tail was swinging slowly, and her eyes were soft. Urgand's gaze smoldered with all the passion and conviction Arcanthus had come to expect from him; however rough Urgand appeared, he cared with immense depth.

She placed a clawed hand on the vorgal's bicep. "You do not need to fight for me, Urgand."

"No, I don't. But I'll happily fight alongside you."

Her lips peeled back in her ilthurii smile. "And I am glad for it."

"Well then"—Arcanthus clapped his hands together, calling his companions' attention to him—"since all that is settled, I'm going to go shower and change."

Urgand nodded. "Getting some sleep?"

Arcanthus's brow furrowed. "What? No. We're going out."

Sekk'thi cocked her head. "You said this is not the day."

Stepping up to them, Arcanthus patted his friends' shoulders. "But that doesn't mean we have nothing to do." Slipping between the pair, he strode toward the master bedroom. "You should make yourselves presentable. I doubt the people of this city would appreciate a nearly naked vorgal parading around the streets."

"Why not?" Sekk'thi asked.

"Yeah, why not?" Urgand demanded, running his hands over his broad chest and down his stomach. "I'm not so hard to look at, am I?"

As he opened the bedroom door, Arcanthus glanced back. "Not at all. But one look in your eyes, and they'd be instantly turned off by your utter lack of charisma."

"I do not think most people would be focused on his eyes." Sekk'thi said, her voice a little lower, a little huskier.

Urgand responded with laughter, but his gaze heated.

Fuck.

Arcanthus missed Samantha more than ever in that moment. He'd passed another night without her, and another morning had come, and he wasn't waking in his bed with his mate nestled against him. Today would be another day without running his hands, mouth, and tongue over her delectable little body, without tasting her, without sliding his cock inside her. Without finding comfort and passion in her arms and providing her the same.

Another day without her smile, her laughter, her voice.

He stepped into the bedroom, closed the door, and brought

up his holocom. He typed out a message as he walked to the bathroom.

No matter how many worlds I see, no matter how many of their people I meet, one thing always remains constant, Samantha...

You. You are the most beautiful thing my eyes could ever behold. You are forever the center of my universe.

I will always be drawn to you.

EIGHT

"And you said no one would want to see," Urgand grumbled as he, Arcanthus, and Sekk'thi walked past a cheering crowd that had gathered around a group of street performers.

None of those performers—males and females of various species, though most were terran—wore anything beyond a pair of undergarments. In fact, several of them didn't even have that much on, instead using the string and percussion instruments strapped over their shoulders to hide their genitalia. Together, the group was singing, playing music, and dancing.

Much to the delight of many onlookers, of course.

"Perhaps it's some obscure terran tradition," Arcanthus suggested.

"Oh?" Urgand chuckled. "I thought you knew everything about terrans."

"More than you, at least."

"I do not believe that is a very high standard of measurement," said Sekk'thi.

Urgand barked laughter, catching the attention of several nearby people—no minor feat considering that the residents of

New York City seemed at least as aloof as those of Arthos, if not more so. "It really isn't."

Arcanthus quickened his pace. "Come along. We aren't here to sightsee."

"He doesn't like being wrong, does he?" Urgand asked Sekk'thi in a loud whisper.

Sekk'thi snickered.

"Oh, you will pay, vorgal," Arcanthus muttered. "You will pay."

"What did you say?" Sekk'thi asked.

"Nothing. We're nearly at our first destination." Arc pointed at a row of elegant storefronts ahead, most of which boasted clean, minimalist designs.

"Maybe I'll go back to the hotel," said Urgand. "The room could use more guarding, right?"

"No, no, vorgal. You're here as part of my personal security detail. What would Drakkal say if he learned you abandoned me in a crowded downtown district of an alien city?"

"That he would have done the same?" Sekk'thi asked.

Arcanthus winced and glanced back at her. "I'm not sure what stings more—the earnestness with which you said that or the fact that you're probably right."

Urgand grinned, his lower lip stretching around his short tusks. "Not *probably*, sedhi."

When they reached the first store, Arcanthus entered without hesitation. Sekk'thi followed close behind. Urgand, unsurprisingly, lingered outside, his amused grin having been replaced by a strained expression.

A female terran with a dark blazer over a white blouse greeted Arcanthus, introducing herself as Christine, and asked if Arc required assistance; he simply shook his head and set about browsing the wares. Sekk'thi remained nearby, her eyes wide and her movements cautious. She'd worn an ilthurii-style wrap today, comprised of several layers of long, silky fabric around her chest, waist, shoulders, and neck that formed something like a dress. The loose, colorful cloth flowed around her gracefully as she moved.

Sekk'thi's dress was simple but elegant, traditional and yet eye-catching. It was strange seeing her in something other than the military style clothing she and the rest of the security team favored back home, but she wore it well. The dress, along with Arcanthus's casual suit, fit in perfectly with the clothing of the professionals they'd passed outside.

Finally, Urgand entered the shop. Amidst the glass shelves and etched crystals, the vorgal looked terribly out of place. His black boots, drab pants, and plain gray shirt might have blended in perfectly on a military base or in a rowdy bar, but here he just looked like an accident waiting to happen.

Christine's eyes widened when they fell upon the vorgal, and the smile she'd given to Arcanthus not a minute before was nowhere to be found. She approached Urgand with startling assertiveness. "Sir, I'm going to have to ask you to—"

"Look at these," Arcanthus called, waving the vorgal over to a collection of crystals. "Don't you think this would be perfect in the foyer?"

With a muttered *excuse me*, Urgand stepped around the terran to join Arcanthus. Though his eyes shone with relief and gratitude, his furrowed brow and clenched jaw suggested confusion and irritation. Arcanthus could almost hear the vorgal's unspoken question.

What the fuck is a foyer?

"Hmm..." Urgand folded an arm across his chest and curled his other fist beneath his chin as he stared at the wares on display. "Not sure. The, uh...novelty would probably wear off quick."

Arcanthus brought a hand up and tapped his lower lip. "I don't know. Crystals have a certain...timelessness, do they not?"

Christine's eyebrows fell. She huffed softly, but she did not press the matter further. Arcanthus watched her with his third eye as she retreated. Though she busied herself by cleaning one of the glass shelves, she regularly cast glares toward the vorgal—and toward Arcanthus as well.

"The fuck we doing here?" Urgand asked under his breath. "Some kind of angle to find new info?"

Crouching, Arcanthus examined a tall crystal with an arrangement of Earth flowers etched inside, marveling at the detail and subtle colors. "Just shopping."

"Really, boss?"

"Really, vorgal." Arcanthus offered his companion a smirk. "Welcome to phase two of the plan."

"Buying shit?"

"Oh, my dearest friend." Arcanthus clucked his tongue and shook his head. "Can you not step back to view the larger picture? We're not merely buying shit. We're buying shit *for* Samantha."

Urgand drew in a deep breath through gritted teeth. "That supposed to make this easier for me?"

"Do you like Samantha?" Sekk'thi asked from the opposite side of the display.

The vorgal met her gaze. "Of course I do. She's a friend, obviously. Basically family."

"Good. Then do not complain when her mate is trying to bring her happiness."

"This isn't exactly where I belong."

The ilthurii walked around to stand beside Urgand, brushing her hand down his forearm. "None of us belongs anywhere. Belonging is not a place. It is people. Friends, family."

"What a heartwarming notion," Arcanthus said. That was exactly how he felt with Samantha. He felt it with everyone else on his ragtag little crew, as well, but most especially with her. Home was not a place, but a state of mind.

Nostrils flaring, Urgand glanced around the store and snickered. "And what a wonderful place to have this conversation."

"Indeed." Arcanthus stood upright. He'd called Samantha his flower, and he'd watched her blossom over the months they'd spent together. This crystal wasn't just a pretty trinket; it would have meaning, symbolism.

And yet...

He lifted his gaze to find Christine approaching.

"You're going to need to make a purchase," she said, "or I will have to ask you three to leave."

"Will you?" Arcanthus frowned, dipped a hand into his pocket, and plucked out a credit chip. "That hardly seems like a good way to treat prospective customers."

Christine pressed her lips together. Whatever else Arcanthus might've said about her—and there was a lot he could've said—she had backbone.

"My friends, would you mind stepping outside?" he asked.

"No fucking problem." After a final glare at the terran, Urgand turned and walked toward the door. Sekk'thi lingered briefly before following him.

Christine stared at Arcanthus pointedly. "This is a prestige establishment. Each and every piece is a work of art, painstakingly designed and crafted by elite artisans. No two are alike. I assure you, sir, that there's nothing here you can aff—"

Arcanthus brushed a thumb over the credit chip, activating the small holo readout that displayed the amount of credits stored on it.

The terran's mouth fell open, her eyes rounded, and she made a soft sound that barely qualified as a whimper.

Closing his fist around the chip, Arcanthus tilted his head. "What was your name again?"

She blinked and cleared her throat. "Christine."

"Well, Christine, I'm currently away from my mate, and I refuse to return to her without gifts in hand. I want something unique for her, something that's one of a kind. Perhaps even a collection of such items. Because there is no one like her."

"W-we... Of course. We have a varied selection, and we can even submit customized orders, if you'd like something more personalized or special." She gestured to one of a few tables arranged at the back of the store; a second employee sat at another table with a customer, filling out information on a holo screen.

Christine continued, "If you'll have a seat, we can review the options."

He nodded and waved her onward, falling into step behind her as she walked to the table. "I should think a set of a dozen would suffice. As a start, anyway."

Her stride faltered. "Absolutely! Whatever you'd like. We can take all the time you need to browse our catalogue. There's much more than what we have on display." Christine rounded the table and pulled out a chair, motioning for him to sit across from her. She wore a wide smile that was made disturbing in that it seemed genuinely warm.

"Perhaps I should've shown the money before you asked my friend to leave?" he asked with a grin.

She laughed—much too quickly and loudly.

"Tell me, Christine... Do you earn commissions based on the pieces you sell?" Arcanthus softened his smile, grasped the chair, and slowly dragged it away from the table.

Christine's smile fell, and her expression sobered. She

tugged down the hem of her blazer and nodded. "We do. To encourage excellence in our service."

With a soft hiss, Arcanthus stilled his hand. "I hadn't realized. In that case"—he pushed the chair back in with the same deliberate slowness, letting the legs scrape on the floor—"I'm afraid I can't do business here."

Again, her eyes rounded, and she raised her palms placatingly. "No, no. It's simply a matter of... Our store has a reputation. An...an image. Your *friend* simply doesn't—"

"You do recall that you're attempting to convince me to do business with you, do you not?"

Her face paled slightly. "I am so, so sor—"

Rage stirred inside Arcanthus's chest. Wealth and power. Everything, everywhere, really did come down to wealth and power, and so much of that was about image. About the façade of sophistication and prestige. Whether it was this place on Earth turning away someone who didn't look refined enough by their standards, or the upper class in Arthos purchasing other thinking beings to keep as pets, servants, and entertainment, whether it was the businessmen and crime bosses who put on their finest before stepping out into public, it was all the fucking same.

And James Clayton was no different. He'd used his means to lure Samantha in, had offered to take care of her, to support her, and then he'd used that power to abuse her, knowing she—a nobody compared to him on the social scale—had no way of combating him.

But this woman wasn't responsible for all that. She was part of it, certainly, but she was simply another part that kept the machine running. Arc's anger was best held in reserve.

He'd have the chance to release it soon enough.

With a nonchalant wave of his hand, he silenced the human. "I'm not the one you should apologize to. Now if you'll excuse me, I'm going to take this shallow victory—because I understand fully that someone like you is not going to change—and leave. Have a wonderful day, Christine."

Arcanthus turned and strode away, leaving the terran sputtering.

Sekk'thi and Urgand were awaiting him when he emerged from the store.

"Guess you feel good about yourself, don't you?" the vorgal asked.

Shrugging, Arcanthus said, "Sometimes self-satisfaction is the only kind available."

"But you did not do that for yourself," said Sekk'thi.

"I didn't?"

"We all know you're not nearly as self-absorbed as you pretend to be," Urgand replied.

Arcanthus arched a brow. "Though I'm not sure why I'd say this aloud, I believe you might be giving me more credit than I deserve, Urgand."

The vorgal grunted. "Klagar's balls. You may be right..."

"There you go again," Sekk'thi said, baring her pointed teeth. "Deflecting."

"And here *we* go again." Arcanthus began walking, falling into the flow of pedestrian traffic.

His companions' rapid footfalls sounded behind him as they hurried to follow.

"Hotel's back that way," said Urgand.

"We've only made one stop," Arcanthus replied. "I've a few dozen more places on our itinerary."

He was out here for Samantha, and he would not be deterred, especially by the likes of Christine from the crystal shop. After his conversation with Abella yesterday, he had a much better idea of what he'd need—of what would help him show his mate just how much he truly loved her.

"Guess I'll be apologizing to Sam when we get back," Urgand said.

"Why?" asked Sekk'thi.

"Because at this rate, I'm going to kill the boss before we make our return trip."

Arcanthus's mouth slanted into a smirk. "I'll try to remember to add your name to the waiting list later, vorgal."

"If you don't put me at the top, we're not friends anymore."

NINE

"You fucking joking?" Urgand glowered at Arcanthus.

Smiling, Arcanthus held the meter-long box a little higher. "Why would I be joking?"

The vorgal's jaw muscles bulged, and the cords popped out along his neck. At least ten bags dangled from his hands and arms already, most of which were full of goods, several long bags containing clothing were draped over his shoulder, and he had a box clamped under each arm.

"You're more than capable of carrying that." Urgand lifted his arms slightly. "And all this too."

"I need my hands free."

"Why? Expecting trouble?" the vorgal asked dryly.

"No." Arcanthus laid the box across Urgand's raised forearms. "Just in case I find anything else I want to purchase." He patted the top of the box and stepped back.

Sekk'thi held her hands out, displaying the fine, pale green scales of her palms. "I will carry some."

"Thank you." Expression softening, Urgand tipped his

head down to pin the clothing bags against his shoulder and turned toward her.

"No," said Arcanthus.

The vorgal glared at him again. "No?"

"Sekk'thi also needs her hands free. She's acting as my bodyguard."

"I'm supposed to be your bodyguard too, not your fucking porter!"

Arcanthus shrugged. "I've decided to alter your job description."

"You can't do that."

"I can. Didn't you read through your employment contract?"

"I did not have to sign a contract," said Sekk'thi.

Urgand's eyebrows fell, combining with his shallow frown to create a decidedly unimpressed expression. "Because there was no employment contract."

Arcanthus pointed a finger at him. "Exactly. So your job is whatever I say it is at any given moment."

Chuckling, Urgand shook his head. "You're slippery as a damned sewer skrudge. This all revenge for me making fun of you earlier?"

Smoothing the front of his suit, Arcanthus replied, "My friend, I am far above such petty retaliation."

"So why have you been making me carry everything all day?"

"Haven't we already been through this?" Arcanthus pressed a hand to his chest. "I have to be able to complete transactions with the merchants." He gestured to Sekk'thi. "She needs to be able to react to danger without her hands being obstructed." Finally, he pointed to Urgand. "And you, vorgal—"

"Have the nicest muscles?" Sekk'thi suggested eagerly.

Arcanthus leveled a flat look at her. "The *biggest* muscles, perhaps, but that doesn't necessarily mean they're the nicest."

"It also does not mean they are not."

"Do I simply not pay the lot of you enough to warrant some flattery every now and again?"

"Sedhi, you're lucky all this stuff is for Sam, or I'd dump it right here and walk away," Urgand said.

"And you're lucky I like you, vorgal." Arcanthus walked toward the store's exit, his tail flicking behind him; it took considerable willpower to keep its movements smooth, to stop it from displaying his restlessness.

He pushed the door open, walked through, and stepped aside, holding it wide.

Urgand slowed as he reached the exit. With a shuffling gait, the vorgal turned and sidestepped through the doorway. His face was a mask of intense focus as he swayed and twisted, narrowly avoiding getting anything caught on the doorframe.

"Who knew you could move with such precision and grace?" Arcanthus asked once Urgand was clear.

Muttering a curse, the vorgal shook his head. Sekk'thi stepped out behind him, her eyes aglow with mirth.

Though the streets were still busy, the crowds had thinned, allowing Arcanthus and his companions space to breathe—and the opportunity to better absorb their surroundings. The similarities between New York and Arthos had been in the macro, in the overall feel and impression. But upon closer examination, the two cities were, unsurprisingly, quite different.

So much here was sleek, shiny, and bright, so much was modern. Metal, glass, and plastic, holograms and lights, electronic displays and fast, efficient public transportation. And it was all juxtaposed by the foundations of the city, by its bones. There was a great deal of stonework all over. Many of the buildings had carved entryways and window frames, sculpted adornments, or brick walls and wooden doors. History was on display here in a way that wasn't common in the Infinite City.

And it served as a sobering reminder to Arcanthus. A mere hundred and fifty years ago, traveling beyond Earth's orbit had been nothing more than a dream to the terrans. Samantha's ancestors from only a few generations prior had looked up at the night sky and seen the unreachable.

Any delay in terran advancement would've been enough to ensure Arcanthus and Samantha had never met. So many events had to have occurred in exactly the right way for him to find her, and the odds of Arc and his mate meeting each other had been so inconceivably low that they bordered on impossibility.

Fuck. I miss her.

"We've been at this all day," Urgand said. "How many more places on your damned list?"

Arcanthus lifted a single finger.

Urgand released a ragged, relieved sigh and uttered thanks to whatever higher powers were listening.

"You're welcome," Arcanthus said before setting into motion and waving his companions along.

They worked their way down the street, passing more shops and businesses. A theater with a large marquee stood across the roadway; hundreds of people were lined up outside, and the pedestrians simply flowed around them. Overhead, hover vehicles flitted by in long streams, with individual vehicles breaking off to descend at designated landing zones.

A message alert sounded from Arc's holocom. Raising his wrist, he looked down. His heart clenched seeing the message from Samantha.

I miss you.

He bared his teeth with a snarl and forced himself to look away from those three little words. She was hurting, far more than that brief message could convey. Everything inside him screamed to return to her side. If she only knew how much he missed her in return, how much it killed him to be so far away from her, how much his heart ached at not seeing her smile every morning.

But Samantha was the reason why Arcanthus was here to begin with.

Another alert drew his attention back to the holocom.

Did that sound too clingy? I'm not trying to be. I know you have work to do. It's just that... This is the first time we've been apart like this, and I just really, really miss you, Arcanthus.

Letting out a long, slow breath, he sent a reply to her, each word making his heart constrict a little more. *I feel it too, my flower. Every second of it. Know that no matter what I'm doing, my thoughts are of you. I will speak with you soon...and I will come home as quickly as I am able.*

When the trio reached their destination, Arcanthus said, "Wait out here. Urgand, you have my authorization to take a break"—he pointed at the vorgal—"but only for five minutes. Understood?"

Urgand grinned. "Oh, there's going to be a break, sedhi..."

"Sekk'thi, keep him in line."

"Gladly," she replied.

The vorgal's grin widened.

"I cannot help but feel as though I've set something into motion that I could not have possibly foreseen." Shaking his head, Arcanthus entered the jewelry store.

An armed guard standing just beyond the door greeted him with a curt nod. Arcanthus responded with a nod of his own before slowly sweeping his eyes across the store. Display cases ran around three sides of the room, with more standing in the space between. The dim overhead lights only strengthened the effect of the many free-floating holo spotlights at each case, which made the items inside glitter and sparkle brilliantly.

He recognized some of the designs and materials—a few of them seemed to be almost universal, spanning many cultures across the cosmos. Many more were unfamiliar to him save for their vague sense of...terran-ness.

Brushing back the sides of his suit jacket and slipping his hands into his pockets, Arcanthus strolled deeper into the store, studying the items on display as he passed. The pieces of jewelry were organized by featured stone. He passed lovely purples, stunning blues, vibrant greens, and deep, rich reds, passed diamonds, passed gold, platinum, and silver. But nothing caught his attention until he reached a small section of black opal jewelry.

The stones each bore clouds of color—red, green, blue, yellow, orange—that shimmered and shifted depending on how he looked at them. In some of those opals, the patterns were reminiscent of nebulae and galaxies swirling through the void of space.

A female terran with graying hair approached from the other side of the counter. "Good evening. Is there anything I can help you with?"

Arcanthus offered her a smile. "Yes. I'd like to have a ring made for my mate."

She smiled back. "We have a wide selection here already. Perhaps one of them will match what you're looking for?"

Removing his hands from his pockets, he activated his holocom. "I'm not much of an artist, but"—he opened the images he'd mocked up on his way back to the hotel that morning—"I wanted something like this. Would the movement be possible?"

The jeweler braced a hand on the counter and leaned closer to study the images. Her eyes brightened. "That shouldn't be a problem. Do you have a stone and cut in mind? Diamonds are traditional here on Earth."

He waved a hand nonchalantly. "Too plain. And I'm far more interest in personal meaning than age-old custom." Extending his arm, he tapped the top of the black opal display case. "One of these."

The jeweler brought up a holo screen over the counter, using it to input details as she asked Arcanthus for more specific information. Within minutes, she'd worked up a model of the ring, which she expanded in the air between them.

Arcanthus's expression softened, and something warm and tight wrapped around his heart. "Perfect."

Smile widening, the jeweler said, "This one will certainly be unique. I can't wait to see the finished piece." She went through a few more menus as the holographic model slowly rotated. "It should be done within two weeks."

"Hmm. I'm going to need it much sooner than that."

"That's our standard turnaround for custom orders, sir, and I assure you, the quality and craftsmanship are worth a far longer wait."

Arcanthus nodded, raking his gaze over the black opals again. "I'll need it in three days."

"Sir, that's—"

"My mate left Earth to seek a new life. She didn't have an easy time here. But it didn't break her, and she's held on to her good memories. To the happiness she had. I'll be returning to her soon, and it is very important that I have this to give her when I get there. Both as a symbol of my love for her and as a reminder of where she came from."

He removed a credit chip from his pocket and set it on the counter, sliding it toward the jeweler. "If you could find a way to expedite the process, it would mean a great deal to me, and even more to her. Far more than I could ever express in words."

Arcanthus returned his hand to his pocket.

The terran let out a slow breath and stared down at the credit chip. She pressed her lips together, and a tiny crease appeared between her eyebrows, but she finally placed her hand over the chip and picked it up. "I'll do everything I can."

"Thank you," Arcanthus said. "Truly."

They finished the order, and Arcanthus produced another credit chip to pay for the bill in full.

His steps were lighter as he exited the store, and anticipation fluttered in his belly. He was excited to see the real thing once it was completed. More than that, he was excited to see Samantha's reaction to it.

TEN

"We're done?" Urgand asked.

Smiling, Arcanthus stepped closer to his friend. He took the long clothing bags off the vorgal's shoulder, draping them over his own arm, and then collected the boxes—both the one that had been held across Urgand's chest and those beneath his arms.

The vorgal's brow furrowed. "Uh..."

"We're heading back to the hotel," Arcanthus said as he hooked a finger through the handles of a few of the bags dangling from Urgand's hand and slid them free.

Sekk'thi cocked her head. "I believe there was a gift shop attached to the hotel lobby."

"Please don't give him any ideas," Urgand said.

Arcanthus's smile widened. "Now that you mention it, Sekk'thi..."

"Don't you fucking dare, sedhi."

Arcanthus and Sekk'thi laughed, and the three made their way to one of the designated landing areas, where they hailed a cab. Once they were all in and Arcanthus had given the autonomous vehicle their destination, Urgand leaned back in his seat and sighed.

Sitting across from the vorgal and the ilthurii, Arcanthus activated the recording blocker before he sank into a comfortable slouch and studied his companions.

He'd known Sekk'thi and Urgand for years. Both had begun as little more than hired guns, necessitated by the nature of his business and the sorts of people he normally dealt with. Thargen, the other vorgal on the crew, had recommended Urgand; the two had fought together in their people's elite military force, the Vanguard.

As for Sekk'thi…her journey hadn't been quite so simple, her path not quite so linear. That she'd emerged from her past to be so easygoing and kind was a wonder. She had every right to be bitter and hateful.

Arcanthus trusted both of them, and he enjoyed their company. He couldn't imagine his life without Urgand, Sekk'thi, and the rest of his friends back on Arthos being part of it.

"Thank you," Arcanthus said.

Both Urgand and Sekk'thi looked at him with confused expressions, though the ilthurii's was understandably subtler.

"For what?" Urgand asked.

"For carrying the bags. For looking out for me. For coming along on this trip." Arcanthus shrugged, lifted a hand, and swept loose hair back from his face. "For everything."

Urgand chuckled, but there was a gentleness in his amusement. "I wouldn't do any of it if you didn't pay so well."

"I'm trying to have a touching moment here, vorgal. Do you always have to ruin things?"

"Only your things, sedhi."

Arcanthus huffed and let his head fall back onto the headrest. "This is what I get for putting Drakkal in charge of security. A team of people who enjoy insulting me."

Sekk'thi bowed her head. Her voice was solemn as she said, "Thank you. I would have remained lost and alone without you. You gave me a home. A family."

"And clearly that family has traumatized you so deeply that you've come to believe joining it was a good thing."

Urgand kicked Arcanthus's shin with a heavy boot, producing a dull, metallic *clank* that vibrated into the sedhi's bones. "Supposed to be having a moment here, remember?"

Arcanthus snickered. "I remember. My apologies, Sekk'thi."

She lifted her head and bared her teeth in a grin. "It is fine."

One corner of the vorgal's mouth shifted back. "This trip really does have you all out of sorts, doesn't it?"

"I've had a great deal on my mind as of late. I suppose I've simply grown more willing to share my thoughts."

"Well, while you're in the sharing mood..." Urgand lifted his chin toward the rear of the vehicle. "What's all the stuff for?"

"Samantha," Arcanthus replied. "Did I not make that clear enough?"

"You can be more specific than that, sedhi."

"Not sure what you mean."

"You are planning something," said Sekk'thi. "No simple gift."

Arcanthus chuckled, shaking his head. "I am. My take on a terran tradition, one I hope to honor in a way that my mate will appreciate."

"Anything you do for her, she will appreciate." Sekk'thi tapped her chest with a loose fist. "She loves you."

"And I love her. Hence my drive to achieve perfection despite knowing I will always fall short of it."

Urgand grinned and glanced at the ilthurii. "Maybe we should ask for pay increases while his guard is down."

Arcanthus arched a brow. "And maybe I should start charging you for room and board, vorgal."

They laughed, and for a little while, Arcanthus was content. But as the cab neared the hotel, he could not prevent his thoughts from darkening.

The surprise he was planning for Samantha filled him with far more excitement than anxiety, and it would've been more than enough on its own to have warranted this trip to Earth. But it wasn't the reason he'd come.

He and his companions shared the burden when they arrived at the hotel, though Arcanthus said he'd carry all of it himself. As they rode the elevator to their floor, he found it impossible to think of anything but time—the time he and Samantha had spent apart, the time left until their reunion. The time he'd spent buying things that held no meaning or value to him without her. The time it took for the elevator to make its ascent.

The time James Clayton had been afforded to live in peace despite his wrongdoings, and however much of that time remained before his cycle of abuse was finally, irreversibly ended.

Arc's melancholy swiftly turned to rage.

The trio entered their suite and set down the bags and boxes, almost covering the table entirely.

"Fuck," Urgand grunted, rolling his shoulders and stretching his back. "This is worse than the first day I had to march wearing full kit."

"You are exaggerating," said Sekk'thi.

The vorgal laughed. "Easy for you to say. Remind me how much you carried for most of the day?"

"I carried the burden of maintaining our security."

"Damn. You're getting good at giving out tongue lashings, Sekk'thi."

"I do not know if that is true, but my tongue is good for a great many other things." Her eyes dipped, and her smile grew.

Urgand's cheeks darkened. "Well fuck."

A gentle vibration coursed up Arcanthus's arm. He glanced down at the holocom built into his prosthesis. The display showed that a new message had been received.

He unlocked the screen.

No name, no comm ID. Just a single, powerful word —*Found.*

Arcanthus's heart skipped a beat, and heat spread outward from it to suffuse his body.

"We, uh..." Urgand cleared his throat. "We should go get something to eat. Been a long day."

A second silent, unidentified message came through. *Scouting tomorrow. Info to come.*

"Yes, we should," Sekk'thi replied. "Perhaps we can go to the place a few streets over? I have wanted to try a *handbirter* since we saw the restaurants on the space station."

Arcanthus drew in a deep breath. Soon, the reason he'd made this trip would be fulfilled. Soon, he would ensure his mate was not only safe, but free from her past.

Urgand frowned. "*Handbirter?*"

"Some sort of terran food," Sekk'thi said. "I may be pronouncing it incorrectly. I have seen many signs for them."

"Whatever you want, I'm willing to try it." The vorgal shifted his gaze to Arcanthus. "You need to change or shower before we go?"

Arcanthus dismissed the holocom screen and shook his head. "I'm not going. But you two should. Enjoy your hamburgers."

Sekk'thi's tail swung enthusiastically. "That is the word! *Hamburger.*"

"Still doesn't mean a damn thing to me," Urgand said with a chuckle. "You sure you don't want to come, boss?"

"I am," Arcanthus replied.

"Not going to disappear on us, right?"

With a chuckle of his own, Arcanthus said, "Not tonight. I simply need some time to think."

"We will bring back hamburger for you," Sekk'thi said.

Arcanthus thanked her, and she and Urgand took their leave. Arc was immediately aware of just how alone he was in that moment, and that only made his situation more dire, more real.

He'd crossed the universe to kill someone—and now that distance separated him from his mate. Not only had James Clayton inflicted physical, mental, and emotional harm upon Samantha during their time together, harm that she still carried in her heart, but he'd now forced Arcanthus away from her.

And Arc felt every centimeter of the distance between himself and Samantha. Nothing else was important now—not the weariness encroaching on the edges of his consciousness, not his self-appointed mission, not the risks and obstacles awaiting him. He needed her.

Sweeping off his suit jacket, he tossed it onto a chair, turned, and strode into the master bedroom. His hand was already up, fingers navigating his holocom, before he willed it to move. Calling her didn't require thought; his body knew. His heart and soul knew.

The display screen read *Connecting...*

He filled his lungs, held the breath, and stared at the screen.

Need you, my flower. I need you.

ELEVEN

Though Arcanthus's heart gained speed with each beat, every second stretched infinitely longer than the last, and the heat gathering inside him was becoming unbearable. He paced the length of the bedroom back and forth, back and forth.

And still the screen only said *Connecting*.

His throat constricted, and his breaths grew strained. His eagerness was becoming anxiety; he needed to hear her voice, to see her face, but she wasn't answering. Was something wrong? If she'd been harmed, if she'd been in danger and he wasn't there to protect her...

The fabric of his shirt felt suddenly too restrictive. Keeping his holocom raised, he clawed at the buttons, tearing off the top two in his desperation to have them open, to breathe. But even with the shirt loosened, he couldn't draw in quite enough air to fill his lungs.

Is she all right?
Is she safe?
Why isn't she answering?

Another second—another eternity—passed, and Arcanthus

could not stand one more. He reached for the control screen. He'd call Drakkal. He had to know, had to be certain everything was okay. That they were okay. That *she* was okay.

But the control screen blinked away, and Samantha's smiling face appeared.

"Arc!" Her gaze flicked over him, and her smile faded. "Are you okay?"

His heart stuttered, and the breath fled his lungs in a relieved exhalation. His skin tingled with the aftermath of his worry. "Fine, Samantha. I'm fine."

She leaned closer to her holocom's receiver and softly asked, "Are you sure?"

Of all the people he'd met, all the relationships he'd formed, no one could calm him like she did. No one could quiet his inner turmoil like his Samantha.

"Is that him?" Drakkal asked from somewhere out of view.

Arcanthus frowned. "Drakkal is there with you?"

Samantha chuckled and shifted, allowing Arc to see Drakkal standing behind her with his arms folded across his chest and his eyes narrowed.

"Well, since you stole Sekk'thi, Drakkal has been my new sparring partner." She wrinkled her nose. "He's not as forgiving."

"Azhera, if you leave even the tiniest mark on her, I'm taking off your other arm," Arc growled.

Drakkal snorted. "Guess it's a good thing for me that you're away on *business* then, isn't it, sedhi?"

Arcanthus glared at him. "You and I will speak when I return."

"We certainly will. But it's not going to go how you want it to."

"You couldn't possibly know how I want it to go." Arc

waved his hand. "Now begone. I called my mate, not my housecat."

Drakkal shook his head. "That one's going to hurt later."

"Good. Perhaps you'll pause to consider the repercussions before you hurl insults at me in the future."

"I didn't mean it's going to hurt me, sedhi."

Arcanthus rolled his eyes. "Oh no, are the *claws* going to come out?"

"I'm just going to take this somewhere private," Samantha said, glancing over her shoulder at Drakkal, who bared his fangs before she walked away, removing him from the frame.

"You're not getting out of this, Arc," Drakkal called.

"It was wonderful talking to you, too, Drakkal," Arc replied.

"He isn't happy that you're gone," Samantha said when she entered the corridor.

"He isn't happy about a lot of things, but he knows as well as I do that this is necessary." For the first time since her holographic image appeared, Arcanthus really looked at his mate, studying every little part of her face and absorbing her beauty anew.

Her hair was gathered in a messy bun atop her head, her cheeks were slightly flushed, and she wore a tank top, baring her shoulders, arms, and upper chest. Those big brown eyes were just as warm and expressive as ever, and they once more possessed a hint of worry.

"Are you sure you're okay, Arcanthus?" she asked. "You didn't look fine before."

He opened his mouth to reassure her, but the words didn't come out. He'd had to hide enough from her regarding this trip; why hide more? "To be honest, my flower, I just needed to see you. And when you didn't answer, I could not stop myself from imagining a thousand horrors that must've befallen you because I am not there with you."

"I'm so sorry. We had the music turned up, which is why I didn't hear your call. But we're okay. Drakkal is on top of everything, and Kiloq, Koroq, and Razi have been picking up the slack. Thargen is... Well, Thargen is Thargen." She smiled. "We're safe. *I'm* safe."

He could not help but smile in return. "I know. You don't need to apologize, Samantha. Rather hypocritical of me to panic when you don't answer immediately considering how often I've been out of contact during this trip." He looked her over again, and his smile softened. "But all that matters is I can look into your eyes now and hear your sweet, sweet voice."

Her cheeks darkened. "I'm happy to see you too. I miss you." She looked away and raised her other arm, opening what Arc assumed to be their bedroom door. "How much longer are you going to be gone?"

Arcanthus walked toward the bed. "I don't know, my flower. Hopefully, we'll depart in a few more days, but I cannot say for sure. However long, I can't get home soon enough."

The background behind Samantha was familiar as she made her way farther into their room, her image shaking as she climbed onto their bed. Once she'd settled herself with her back against the headboard, knees drawn up, and arm resting upon them, she smiled. "I can't wait for you to get home too. And you still can't tell me where you are?"

"Not yet, Samantha."

Her brow creased, her eyes dipped, and a small laugh escaped her. "Arc, are you wearing a dress shirt?"

Frowning, he looked down and pinched the fabric of his shirt, pulling it open slightly. "I'm just trying to avoid standing out. Are you going to make fun of me for it too?"

Samantha shook her head. "Oh, no! No, I wouldn't make

fun of you. It's just...different. I've only ever seen you wearing robes and loincloths. Or, well, nothing at all." Catching her bottom lip between her teeth, she tilted her head down and peered up at him. "You do look handsome in it though."

"Of course I do," he purred as tantalizing heat flared in his belly. His hand crept back up to his shirt, fingers teasing the next button. "But it is rather warm here."

Her gaze fixated on his fingers. "Is it?"

He unfastened the button and spread the shirt open a little more. "Desperately so."

"Maybe you would be more comfortable...taking it off?"

Arcanthus grinned. "My, Samantha, how brazen you've become."

Her eyes widened, and she ducked her head, covering her face with her hand. "Only because you bring it out in me." She spread her fingers to look through them. "This is a lot like the first time we ever talked over holocom."

His grin widened, and he undid another button. "Oh, I can think of a few ways it's different."

"How so?"

"I didn't snap at you after mistakenly thinking you were one of my employees, for one." Another button undone, and his hand dipped toward his waist. "And I haven't seen your panties yet."

"You haven't..." She dropped her hand and gaped at him. "You saw my panties?"

"Yes. Lovely white ones." An appreciative growl rose in his throat at the memory. "That luscious ass of yours occupied my thoughts far more often than I'd care to admit afterward."

"I didn't know you could see them from that angle."

"Oh, I did. And it was the most delightful torture I've ever endured." The last button gave way, and he spread his shirt to the sides. "Let down your hair, my flower."

Eyes on his chest, Samantha reached up and pulled her hair tie free. Her long brown hair cascaded around her shoulders. She shook her head, allowing the locks to settle.

"Ah, my mate, how is it that you grow more beautiful with each passing day?" Arcanthus rasped. His cock strained against the inside of his slit, pulsing with a deep ache.

Her cheeks flushed. "You make me feel it."

"All I've ever done is point out what's always been there." He slipped his shirt off, letting it pool on the bed behind him as his gaze fell to the gentle slopes of her breasts. "Let me see more of that beauty."

Samantha looked down and wrung her hands. "I've... I've never done this before, Arc."

"Perhaps not, but we've done so much more together." He leaned closer to her image. "Look at me, Samantha."

She met his gaze without hesitation.

"I would never force you to do anything you are uncomfortable with." He reached out to brush the backs of his fingers over her cheeks. When they only passed through the hologram, he curled them into a fist and lowered his hand. That he could not comfort her with something as simple as a touch was infuriating. "You are safe with me. You know that, right?"

She nodded, her eyes glimmering with emotion. "I do."

"I will always wait for you to take that leap toward me. Though we're far apart, I am here with you. These moments are ours to seize, ours to define. And I want only to spend them with you. I don't care how."

"Arc..." Her brow furrowed, and she gripped the collar of her tank top. "It's not that I'm uncomfortable. I *want* to do this with you. It's just something new, and I'm... I'm nervous. Nervous that it won't be what you're expecting, that I won't be any good at it. That'd I'll...disappoint you."

His expression softened, and he let out a gentle sigh. "Ah,

my flower. You could never disappoint me. To me, everything you do is perfect. *You* are perfect."

Her eyes searched his. "I wish you were here. I wish I could touch you."

"I wish the same." He tilted his head, and his lips spread in a slow grin. "Until then, we will have to act as each other's hands." He shifted until his back was against the headboard, flicking his finger to fix the hologram in the air and placing down an optical receptor disc before him to free his arm. "Where would you touch me, my mate?"

"Your lips." She brought her fingers to her mouth and brushed them across her bottom lip. "I'd kiss them."

He mimicked her action with his own hand. Though it could never match the feel of her fingers on his lips, a tingle spread across them all the same. "Your kiss never fails to ignite a fire in me. What would you do next?"

She worried her lower lip as her eyes moved over him. "I... I'd run my hands over your chest. I'd feel your heat beneath my palms, feel your heart beating."

Arc trailed his hands over his pecs, stopping one over his heart just as Samantha placed her hand over hers.

"I'd feel it pounding in tandem with mine," she said softly, eyes meeting his. "What would you do to me?"

His cock pushed out of his slit and was halted by the barrier of his pants, nearly making him shudder. "I would peel off your clothing, baring you to me a little at a time. Barely maintaining control, but unwilling to let the moment pass too quickly."

Samantha's fingers curled against her chest. She took in a deep inhalation and slowly released it as she sat up and brought her holocom closer. A moment later, she leaned forward, and when she scooted back against the headboard, the optical receptor she'd positioned at the end of the bed granted Arcanthus full view of her.

"Okay, Samantha," she whispered to herself as she grasped the bottom of her tank top. "Sexy. You can be sexy."

Arcanthus's heart melted. *You are.*

She drew her shirt over her head, revealing her belly and her sports bra, and tossed it aside. With her head bowed and her long hair draped over her shoulders, she worked the straps of the bra off until that garment followed the other.

Arcanthus watched raptly as his mate undressed. He watched her pink nipples harden in the open air, watched her shield herself with her arms before she bravely forced them away, watched her grip the waistband of her leggings. Though her movements were by no means those of an experienced seductress, Arc was utterly enticed; he couldn't have looked away even if he'd wanted to.

His cock throbbed, and there was a deep ache in his groin, one that would not be soothed until he had Samantha back in his arms.

She lifted her ass as she shoved her pants and underwear off her hips and down her legs. With the cuffs of her leggings caught around her feet, Sam paused and looked at Arcanthus with a shy expression. "I...guess that wasn't exactly slowly peeling my clothes off, was it?"

Unable to keep a hungry growl from his voice, Arc replied, "It was perfect, Samantha."

She smiled and shook her head as she tugged the garments off her feet. "You're just saying that."

"No, my flower. I'm feeling it." He drew in a shaky breath and clenched his teeth at the pressure in his groin. His shaft strained against his pants, demanding freedom, demanding her warmth, her touch.

Settling back into place with her legs curled to one side, she swept her hair over one shoulder and nervously combed her fingers through the long strands. "Will you undress for me too?"

The corner of his mouth ticked up. "My hands are yours. Tell me what you would do, Samantha."

"I'd...I'd..." She closed her eyes and pressed her lips together, as though fortifying herself. "While my lips and tongue are tracing your qal, I'd run my hands down your stomach, curling my fingers so that my nails graze your skin." She opened her eyes. "Then I'd tease you, just above your pants, running my fingers back and forth."

His abdominal muscles twitched as he followed her guidance, trailing his hands over his skin. The tingling sensation produced by his touch was tantalizing, enhanced by the desire in her eyes.

"And then I'd open your pants to release you," she continued.

He practically tore the fabric apart in his eagerness to claim that freedom, and he sucked in a sharp breath as the cool air teased the heated flesh of his shaft. His tendrils writhed, eager for her warmth, yearning for release. He clenched his pants with both fists to keep from grabbing himself.

Samantha's gaze locked on his cock. Her tongue slipped out to wet her lips—lips Arc was desperate to take, to kiss, to taste. Her fingers had stilled in her hair, gripping the strands the way he always did.

"I would stroke my thumb across your lip." He briefly caught his own lip with a fang as he watched her bring her fingertips to her mouth. "Then slowly down your chin and along your slender throat before taking your breasts in my hands and claiming you with a searing kiss."

Eyes darkening and lips parting, she cupped her breasts.

"Squeeze them, Samantha. Caress them. Worship them as I would. Just like that. Imagine my mouth capturing one of those pretty nipples, sucking hard, imagine my fangs teasing your tender flesh."

She pinched her nipple, twisted it, and whimpered. "Arc…"

"What is it, my flower? What is it you want?"

"I want you."

"And you have me. In every way possible, even a universe apart. Now spread your legs and let me see you."

Lifting one of her knees, she slowly dropped it aside, parting her thighs. Her sex opened to reveal its pink petals, already coated with the dew of her arousal.

Arcanthus groaned, his tail thumping hard on the bed. His pants ripped as the tension in his arms intensified tenfold, but he did not allow them to move any farther. "Fuck, Samantha. You're already wet for me."

Her cheeks flushed, but she didn't stop caressing her breasts. "Wrap your hand around your…your…"

He grinned. "My cock?"

She nodded.

Arcanthus forced one hand to release his pants. How was it possible for a cybernetic limb to feel stiff and strained? Slowly, he shifted that hand to the base of his shaft and closed his fingers around it. The tendrils drew together. A shudder coursed through him, wringing a growl from his throat, and he squeezed tighter, desperate to halt the inevitable explosion.

"Stroke it," Samantha said. "Slowly, as I would."

Without breaking eye contact with her, Arc slid his hand up. He drew in a harsh breath through his nostrils and gritted his teeth at the overwhelming sensation, but he didn't stop, didn't alter that deliberate pace. "Slide your hand down, my flower. Tease yourself as you move it toward your pussy, just as I would."

Releasing one of her breasts, Samantha skimmed her fingers over her belly, circling her navel, then farther down, crossing the patch of dark curls Arc loved to pet until she reached the apex of her sex.

"Stop there," Arc rasped, voice quivering as he continued stroking. "Tell me, Samantha. Tell me what you want, what you need."

"I want you to touch me. I...I want your mouth, your tongue, your fingers."

"But all you can have is my voice. My command."

Something flickered in Samantha's eyes, something akin to fear, and her breaths grew rapid. She turned her face away with her brows drawn and eyes closed as she took in one deep breath after another.

"Not him," she whispered so quietly that Arc barely heard it.

Arcanthus stilled his hand, and his heart stuttered. Had he pushed her too fast? Too hard? Had he stirred up some memory, reopened some old wound?

Not him could only refer to one person, but Arc's concern for his mate in that moment far outweighed his hatred of James Clayton.

"Samantha?"

She turned her face toward him. That fear that had been in her eyes was gone, replaced by determination.

Determination and love.

"Command me," she said.

"We can stop." Despite the unbearable pressure in his groin, despite the torturous ache in his cock, he managed to keep his voice steady. His own discomfort was a small price to pay to ensure her wellbeing.

"No. Please, Arcanthus. I...I need this. I need *you*." She spread her legs wider, her finger still positioned above her clit. "Command me. I am yours."

That light in her eyes, once again ravenous, silenced any further doubts he might have had and sent a fresh wave of desire through him. His fingers twitched, squeezing his tender shaft. He barely suppressed a growl.

"Move your hand lower," he said, resuming the pumping of his fist. "Gather your slick upon your fingertips."

He groaned as her middle finger dipped between the folds of her slit and disappear inside her pussy. How he wanted that to be his finger—or his tongue. His mouth watered at the memory of her taste.

"Now circle your clit," he continued, watching her raptly. "Yes. Just like that. Imagine it is my tongue lavishing you with pleasure, gradually building that sensation, just how I know you love it. Controlled despite my eagerness to taste you."

Samantha's lashes drooped, but she didn't close her eyes as she continued pleasuring herself. Her breaths quickened, growing shallower, and her body grew restless. Arc knew she needed more.

"Arcanthus..." she whispered, squeezing her breast. "Please."

"I'm not done enjoying that pussy yet, my flower. I would lick every part of you and thrust my tongue deep, again and again, drinking from that pretty slit." He clenched his jaw, and his nostrils flared as she thrust two fingers into her sex and pumped them. That sensation within his core expanded. Seed seeped from the creases between his tendrils, coating his palm, and he groaned. "Only when you are trembling and on the verge of release would I take your clit between my lips and suck."

She withdrew her fingers, which were now glistening with her slick, returned them to that hard little bud, and stroked. A moan escaped her.

"Faster. Harder." He dropped his hand from his pants, clutching the bedding beneath him as he matched his pace to hers. "Ride your pleasure ever higher, Samantha. I will hear you crying out my name before we are through."

She whimpered as she worked her clit, stroking faster and faster. Nectar dripped from her sex, and the sight only intensified his hunger for her. She writhed, her pelvis undulating in time with her strokes, her thighs quivering, and her toes curled into the blanket.

Her whimpers soon turned into shallow panting and soft moans that called to Arc's bestial side to take. To claim.

To conquer.

He bared his teeth. "Fuck, you are beautiful. Imagine me pushing my cock inside you. Remember the feel of me, filling you, stretching you. Remember the feel of my tendrils worshipping you from within, touching every spot that makes you burn."

"Yes," Samantha breathed. "Yes, I remember. Oh my God, I wish you were here. I want you so bad. I...I... Ah!" She squeezed her eyes shut, and her head fell back against the headboard as she cried out.

"Do not relent," Arcanthus growled through his teeth, body trembling with his imminent climax. Ecstasy coursed through his veins, suffusing his body, and though it was but an echo of what he would've experienced with her in person, he would take it greedily. "Bring yourself to your peak, my flower, and then beyond. Remember my lips on your breasts, my fingers in your hair. Remember our bodies moving in perfect rhythm."

Samantha released her breast to grasp her hair, her cries escalating. She spread her thighs wider. Her fingers quickened, and her hips worked in unison, accelerating her already frantic pace.

The pressure within Arcanthus reached an overwhelming level. Each stroke of his fist should have been his undoing, but release eluded him, and the sensation only built impossibly stronger.

She forced her eyes open and met his gaze an instant before her body stiffened, and it was his name—filled with longing, with pleasure, with passion—that spilled from her lips. That liquid heat he so craved flowed from her. Her thighs clamped together around her hand as her back arched.

"Open them," Arcanthus snarled.

With another desperate cry, she obeyed, forcing her knees apart. Her face was flushed, eyes half-lidded and gleaming with delirious pleasure. "Arcanthus…"

"Take me," Arcanthus commanded, "all of me." His hand blazed down his shaft, and his tendrils opened on a swell of bliss so immense that his hips lifted off the mattress. He roared as his seed erupted to spill hot across his abs and thighs. He gripped the base of his shaft tighter. His entire being pulsed with sensation, but he didn't allow himself to look away from his beautiful mate.

No amount of time or distance would break his bond with her.

All too soon, the pleasure faded, and Samantha's cries fell silent. The two of them sat, panting, and stared at one another. The warmth of their love flowed freely across those unfathomable stretches of space. Arcanthus's heart gradually eased, and the tingling heat beneath his skin dissipated.

Samantha withdrew her hand from between her thighs and crawled closer to the optical receptor. Rising on her knees, she reached out as though to cup his face. Arcanthus leaned toward that holographic touch, and the phantom sensation of her palm against his skin flickered across his cheek. He lifted a hand to do the same, wishing there was something tangible beneath it. Wishing she was with him.

"My flower," he purred.

"I love you."

"And I love you."

"I wish I could feel you." She tilted her head toward his hand. "Come home to me soon."

He smiled softly, unable to keep the expression from being tinged by sorrow. "As soon as possible, Samantha. I'll be counting every single second until I have you in my arms again."

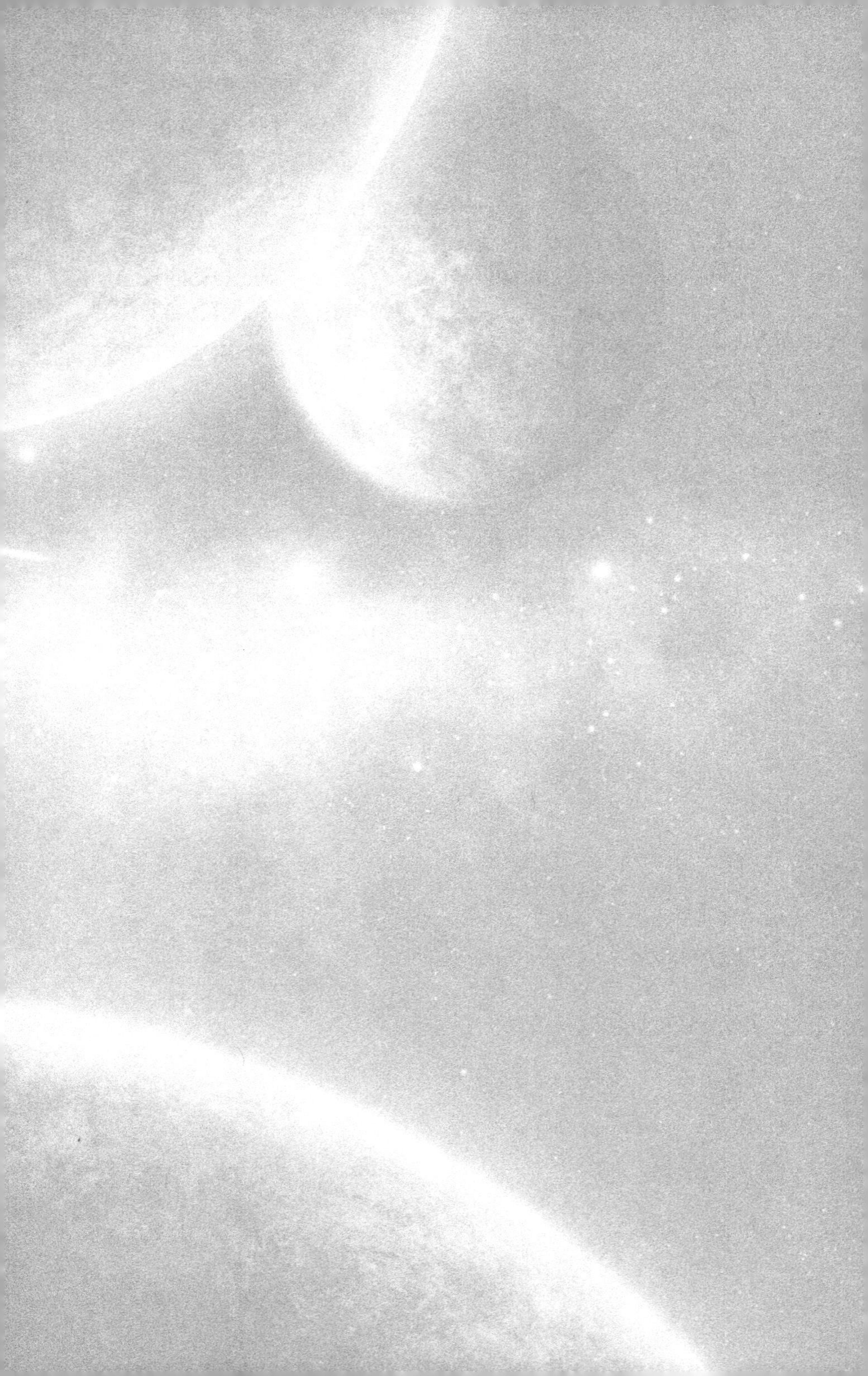

TWELVE

"Be careful," Abella said.

Frowning, Tenthil combed his fingers through her dark hair, grazing her scalp with his claws. "I am always careful."

Her eyebrows rose, and the corner of her mouth quirked in disbelief. "Always?"

He grunted, and a smile spread across his lips. "Often enough. And you wanted me to help him."

Abella sighed and eased closer to Tenthil. She cupped his jaw in both hands, and her beautiful green eyes held his gaze. "It's the right thing to do. But I still want you to come home safe."

"I swear it." He bent down and pressed his lips to hers, fighting back the flow of sweet venom as her taste danced across his tongue and her fragrance filled his nose. He hooked an arm around her middle and tugged her body against his.

Mine.

A low growl rumbled in his chest, and heat surged to his cock, making it throb.

Abella broke the kiss, evading his ravenous mouth with a

subtle shift of her face. She chuckled. "You should probably get going."

Growling again, he closed his fist in her hair and tipped her head back. He drew in a ragged breath. "I smell your arousal, female."

She caught her bottom lip between her teeth and exhaled shakily as she wiggled against his shaft. "And I can *feel* yours."

"Abella," he rasped, nuzzling her hair.

He'd awoken this morning with her backside tucked against his front, and giving in to his desire had been a simple matter of raising her leg and sliding his cock into her welcome heat. Her moans had been the sweetest of sounds. She'd come alive quickly, reaching for him, begging him for more, and he'd used his fingers on her clit and full breasts, bringing her to release twice before seeking his own.

Though her pregnancy had him curtailing his urges to take her with his usual passionate savagery, he truly enjoyed the slow, sensual lovemaking of the last few months. It didn't matter how many times they came together, he'd never have enough of his mate.

"I'm going through my maternity clothes a lot faster than intended thanks to those claws of yours," she said, a husky note in her voice. When he lifted his head, she pecked a quick kiss on his lips and withdrew before he could trap her mouth with his. "And you have work to do, husband."

Tenthil huffed. He lowered his face to her hair again, drew in her scent once more, and released her.

But Abella's hands lingered on his face. "If half of what he said is true, Tenthil, you're helping bring down a bad person. And I don't think any of it was a lie."

"But to risk the life we've made, to endanger you and her—"

She smoothed her hands higher, calming him with her gentle touch. "This man hurt an innocent woman. Someone's daughter, who had a father who cared very much about her but couldn't be there to protect her. He's trying to hurt her more now. And I very much doubt she's the only one he's harmed."

Abella took one of his hands and guided it to her belly. "What if it had been our daughter in her place?"

Tenthil's lips peeled back, baring his fangs, and the sting of venom on his tongue chased away the sweetness of Abella's taste. The heat of his passion flared, growing into a roaring inferno of rage. Just the thought of harm befalling his mate and child was enough to spark his most primal and violent instincts.

Again, it was Abella's touch that soothed his inner beast, this time as she brushed her thumb across his cheek. "Do the job. Keep yourself safe. And come back to me."

He nodded, swallowing the bitter venom.

"Trust me when I say I'll be *eagerly* awaiting your return." Abella grinned, a mischievous light sparking in her eyes as she lowered her hands and backed away from him. Her shirt, made of a light, flowing material, offered him a glimpse of her hard nipples.

Tenthil's cock ached. It took all his willpower to force himself to turn around, and even more to stride to the door. The sensation of her gaze upon his back was nearly enough to break his resolve.

Offering her a wave over his shoulder, he unlocked the door, opened it, and stepped out into the balmy California morning.

Need to go back to her. Protect her.

Rut her.

Shutting his eyes, he paused. Her scent lingered in his nose, and his lips thrummed in the aftermath of their kiss. Today was not a day for him to submit to his instincts, at least not yet. He had business to attend, and once it was concluded, he would be done with the damned sedhi once and for all.

He would be done with the entire city of Arthos once and for all.

The apartment door closed behind him. He opened his eyes and walked along the breezeway, feeling the distance between himself and Abella grow with his every step.

The complex was quiet, with only a few other people outside. That would change as the day wore on. Today was a Saturday, a day of the week many terrans seemed to hold sacred—most of them did not have to work, and children didn't go to school. By midday, dozens of younglings would be outside playing, the pool would be packed, and there'd be at least a few humans grilling food on their barbecues.

Tenthil appreciated the sense of community present during such days even if he had little interest in involving himself. His reluctance was partly because he'd had more than his fill of community, albeit in a much more insidious fashion, during his time in the Order.

But it was also because he couldn't look at all those terrans laughing, talking, and playing without feeling like a predatory beast walking amongst prey that had become too docile to notice the danger in their midst.

He turned into the corridor that led to the parking structure, again battling the instinctual urge to return to his mate.

Going to be a long day.

It was only when he reached the top floor of the garage that he realized the truth of that thought—his hoverbike was parked in its usual spot, but a black hovercar was idling in the air behind it, effectively blocking the smaller vehicle into its sheltered space. The hovercar wasn't one he'd seen here before, and its tinted windows hid the interior from view.

Tenthil clenched his jaw and lowered a hand to his belt, taking hold of the blaster pistol on his hip. A thousand scenarios played out in his mind, all spiraling outward from one notion—the hovercar's placement must've been intentional.

Raking his eyes across the entire level, he advanced toward the unfamiliar vehicle. Stinging venom gathered on the tips of his fangs. His skin thrummed as he altered his bioelectricity to disrupt his appearance on any nearby surveillance cameras.

In his old life, he would've drawn his weapon and fired into the front windshield as he approached. But restraint was often the better choice here on Earth. It wasn't just a matter of protecting his family from physical harm, but of doing all he could to provide them with the security and lifestyle they deserved. It was a matter of providing them peace. He couldn't do that if he was arrested for murder.

The hovercar's antigrav drive hummed. Tenthil felt its faint vibrations in the air even through his clothing.

His insides drew taut as he stepped up to the driver's side door. Firing upon a target from a vehicle was a crude means of assassination, but it had been done often in Arthos—and from what Tenthil understood, it had also been done on Earth over the last two centuries.

Lifting his free hand, he knocked on the window.

The window slid down, revealing the dark interior a centimeter at a time. Tenthil's muscles tensed, ready to burst into action in a fraction of a moment, even as he forced words out of his mouth. "You're blocking me in."

But the driver's seat was empty.

He drew the blaster and took a step back, aiming into the cab; he expected a shot from somewhere else, from the back seat or a nearby building, because this could only be a trap, could only be—

"Do the people of Earth normally shoot each other over such matters, zenturi, or are you just falling into old habits?" someone asked in a familiar voice from inside the vehicle.

Tenthil's gaze fixed on the figure in the passenger seat, whose golden eyes and *qal* glowed in the dim light. "What the fuck, sedhi?"

"People keep saying that," Arcanthus said with a smirk, "but I can never quite tell why."

With blaster raised and finger on the trigger, Tenthil glared at the sedhi. Would it really have been so terrible to shoot now, walk away, and carry on with his life? That certainly would've been safest for Tenthil and his family; no one knew who they were or the truth of their forged IDs but Arcanthus. No one else knew where they were.

Arcanthus sighed, his gaze unwavering. "We're wasting time. Either shoot me or get in."

"You came to our home again," Tenthil growled.

"Where else was I meant to meet you?"

Tenthil bared his fangs, venom trickling over his tongue. "You're putting my family in danger."

"You're the one pointing a gun into my hovercar while standing atop an open-air parking structure." The sedhi cocked his head. "But let me guess—you're using your little trick to stay off surveillance, aren't you?"

Tenthil just continued glaring.

Arcanthus activated his holocom, bringing up a screen and enlarging it. It was a surveillance feed from a holo recorder overlooking this garage, currently showing a black hovercar with the driver's side window down. Only the occasional digital artifact flickering beside the car gave any indication that Tenthil was there at all.

Releasing a slow, heavy breath, Tenthil returned the blaster to its holster. "Don't have the info yet."

"Obviously. That's why I'm here."

Bracing both hands on the window frame, Tenthil leaned down. "Not letting you rush me."

The sedhi laughed and shook his head. "I'm not here to rush you, my friend. I'm here to scout the location with you."

Tenthil's brows fell. He waited for the sedhi to laugh again and say it was a joke, to say he was going to leave Tenthil to his work, but Arcanthus just stared back at him.

"No." Tenthil shoved away from the vehicle. "Out of the way."

"You haven't asked nicely."

"Get the fuck out of the way."

Arcanthus propped an elbow on the central armrest and leaned toward Tenthil. "What have I done to earn such hostility from you, zenturi?"

Tenthil let a silent glower serve as his response.

"Manual controls are engaged," the sedhi said, patting the driver's seat. "Feel free to move it yourself."

Tenthil didn't know an adequate number of curses to hurl at Arcanthus in that moment, not that they would've made a difference. The sedhi could go on like this for a long, long time. The quickest route, though it went against all Tenthil's instincts and desires, was to humor Arc a little.

Perhaps he could drive the hovercar up to a reasonable height, open the passenger door, and shove the sedhi out...

Releasing a low grow, Tenthil opened the door. The hovercar bounced and swayed upon its antigrav field as he climbed in. Surprisingly, the seat was already adjusted to accommodate his height. Arcanthus wasn't much shorter than Tenthil; clearly, the sedhi must've set the seat for himself.

That was what Tenthil wanted to believe, anyway.

Grasping the controls, Tenthil reversed the hovercar, clearing the way for his bike. Once he stopped the vehicle, he slipped a leg out through the open door, planted his foot on the ground, and looked at Arcanthus. "Leave. Do not come back here."

Arcanthus leaned back in his seat and held a palm up. "You're already at the controls, zenturi."

"Sedhi..."

The smug expression faded from Arcanthus's face, and a new light entered his eyes—a dangerous light, calculating but wild at its core. A primal part of Tenthil recognized that light.

"You know my skills will benefit this outing, Tenthil. And I'm the one who'll be doing the deed. I should be there to check it out."

There was something more under the sedhi's words, something Tenthil never would've expected from Arcanthus—true emotion. The sedhi's devotion to his mate, Samantha, wasn't the sort of thing that could be faked. Not when it was so large a part of him that it seemed to have suffused his very soul.

"All I'm asking is for you to put up with me for a few more hours," Arcanthus said, voice low. "Then we're done. You move on and live with your family, a little wealthier, and I eliminate a threat to my mate." He brushed his hands together. "And we never see each other again."

"Fuck," Tenthil snarled, drawing his leg back into the cab. He tugged the door closed, placed his hands on the controls, and stilled, letting out a long, harsh breath.

Why was he going along with this? What was wrong with him?

Through gritted teeth, he asked, "This a rental?"

"Yes."

"We're being tracked."

"Don't worry. I've taken care of all that."

"Why do you need me then?" Tenthil glanced at the sedhi from the corner of his eye. "You could've found him. Could've done all this on your own."

Arcanthus bent a leg, propping his metal foot on the dashboard as he slouched a little further. "I could have. But you have some familiarity with Earth, and experience with work like this. I'm not so arrogant as to believe I know better than everyone. At least not *all* the time."

"Told you I'm not killing anyone."

"And I haven't once asked you to."

"People usually don't ask directly."

"I haven't asked indirectly, either."

"Yet."

"I made a point not to pry regarding your circumstances before, Tenthil, and I certainly won't do so now, but it's clear to me that someone has harmed you in the past, leaving you with crippling trust issues."

Tenthil snickered and shook his head. "You live in a fortress with armed guards and autocannons mounted in your workshop, but I have trust issues?"

Arcanthus leveled a finger at Tenthil. "Firstly, that's no longer the case. I've yet to have the autocannons installed in our new facility. Secondly, all my security is the result of caution, not an inability to trust."

Tenthil's hands tightened on the controls. "Already regretting this."

Arcanthus chuckled. "We're only just beginning, zenturi."

THIRTEEN

The hovercar's controls groaned as Tenthil squeezed them. Tension radiated from him in waves, triggering recognition deep within Arcanthus—his inner beast, the ancient blood of tretin conquerors that coursed through his veins, acknowledging another predator, a potential threat, an inevitable challenger. That only fueled his own restlessness, intensifying the uneasy energy pulsing through his limbs with no distinguishment between flesh and metal.

In a teasing tone that conveyed none of that, Arc asked, "Rather impatient for a master assassin, aren't you?"

Tenthil grunted, glaring at Arcanthus with silver eyes—though that silver was retreating from his expanding pupils. "Not an assassin anymore."

Arcanthus shifted aside a holo screen to make space for a new one, bringing his total up to eight, all of which were arranged in the air before him. "And I haven't been a pit fighter for many years, but I didn't suddenly lose all those skills once I changed careers."

He ran his lower eyes across the other screens, checking the various surveillance feeds they displayed, while keeping his third eye on the new screen. Countless lines of code scrolled across it, most of them in terran characters he didn't fully understand.

"Not an assassin," Tenthil repeated in a growl.

As he brought up a program to translate the code into something he could comprehend, Arc said, "Noted, zenturi. I'll mind my tenses."

"Or just don't talk."

"My apologies, but I'm not in the habit of making promises I can't keep." Arcanthus lifted his attention to look out the hovercar's front window. The place Tenthil had landed the vehicle was perfect—not only did it look downhill directly at James Clayton's home, but it was out of view of the many surveillance systems installed at nearby properties.

The house itself was entirely unchanged from its state when Arcanthus and Tenthil had arrived hours ago. Beneath the gray, overcast evening sky, the property was still but for the swaying of foliage in the breeze. The windows were dark, and the halls and rooms inside were silent and devoid of life. He would've known if anyone was inside; he'd checked through the house's cameras at least a hundred times so far.

James Clayton wasn't home.

But there'd been something in the house's integrated computer system to suggest that would change—the coffee maker was programmed to come on soon.

Tenthil released the controls, folded his arms across his chest, and leaned his shoulder against the door.

Arcanthus sighed, checked the progress on the coding translation, and glanced at his companion. "I would much rather be with my mate right now too. And however little it means to you, you have my sincere thanks for this. I understand what it's like to be separated from someone you love."

Jaw muscles bulging, Tenthil angled his head down, making his pale hair fall to obscure his face. "I feel every moment I'm apart from her. A pain unlike any other."

"Greater than any torture, more agonizing than any wound." Arc nodded, swallowing back a flare of that very pain. "I'd always thought such descriptions of love were overly dramatic."

The zenturi grunted. "I wanted to hate you for this, sedhi." Though his voice grew rougher with every word, he continued. "Hate you for pulling me away from her. But she's right. Without you, we wouldn't have the life we're trying to make."

Arc's smile was shallower than usual, tinged with a hint of melancholy. "I can't exactly claim my motivations were selfless in our dealings."

"Maybe not. And I did want to kill you..."

Arcanthus chuckled. "Unsurprisingly, you were far from the first."

"But I am glad I didn't. Even now."

"Well...thank you. I appreciate it. I only wish I could promise that won't change."

Tenthil let out a harsh breath and said, "You ever show up at my home again, and it will. Instantly."

"Understood. Conversely, if you're ever in Arthos—"

"Won't be."

"Humans have a saying. *Never say never.*" Arcanthus shrugged and returned his attention to the screens.

"Just did."

"So, does your mate find the same thrill in conversing with you that I do?"

"Do you ever take anything seriously?" Tenthil snapped.

"Do you ever not?" Arc swiped his fingers across the latest holo screen, surveying the translated code, which was marked as property of Omni-Forge Security Systems, Incorporated.

With a low snarl, Tenthil raked a hand through his hair, sweeping it back.

Partially realized ideas sparked in the back of Arcanthus's mind as he studied the code, like distant stars flickering into view as night slowly fell. But he didn't pursue any of them. All he really wanted, both consciously and subconsciously, was to be reunited with Samantha. Now.

Yet he understood that dwelling upon that desire would put him in the foulest of moods, and despite his rumbling instincts, he didn't want to fight Tenthil.

"So, zenturi"—he returned his gaze to James Clayton's house—"what is your assessment?"

Tenthil tilted his head and stared at the house. His jaw ticked, and his pupils seemed uncertain as to whether they wanted to expand or contract.

After a long silence, he said, "Private residence, low security. Windows will keep onlookers from seeing inside. If you can deactivate the security system without alerting the company, should be simple to get in." He pointed down. "Climb a tree near the wall and you'd be clear. But most systems will trigger if they lose contact with their main servers."

"Sitting here for how many hours, and that's the plan you've constructed? Climb a tree?"

"You asked for my assessment." Again, Tenthil grasped the controls. "Areas like this, people are watchers. Cameras everywhere, eyes everywhere. That's the main issue."

"My real identity is virtually untraceable."

"But your kind aren't common on Earth. Even if they don't know your name, you'd never get off planet if they knew a sedhi was involved in a murder."

This time, Arcanthus released a harsh breath. "So, your suggestion?"

"Darkness."

Arcanthus stared blankly at his companion. "Darkness."

"Simple, sedhi. This kind of work, simple is almost always better." Tenthil cleared his throat, partly restoring his flagging voice. "Humans see poorly at night. Can't identify you if they can't see you."

Bracing a hand on the dash, Arc drummed his fingers. That the former assassin was right did not bother him, but he could've done without the condescension. Still, he bit back any would-be retorts and instead asked, "How would you do it?"

"My way wouldn't work for you."

Arcanthus raised a palm. "Obviously. And yet I asked all the same."

"I'd watch for a few days. Learn his habits. What time he's home, what time he leaves. When he showers, eats, sleeps. Watch the neighbors too. Then I'd go over the wall in the middle of the night, get inside, and make sure he doesn't wake up the next morning. Leave the same way, but at a different spot."

"And the security system?"

Tenthil shrugged. "Not a concern for me."

"My, that little trick of yours is certainly useful."

"Yes"—Tenthil's brow's knitted—"but I never asked for it."

"Few of us are lucky enough to get what we ask for." Arcanthus saw Samantha, so small, so sweet, so kind and beautiful, in his mind's eye. "Fewer still are fortunate enough to keep it."

"Crossing the universe to protect her is not fortune, sedhi. It is devotion. It is love."

Yes. Yes, it is.

If Tenthil's method was out of the question, Arcanthus would have to find his own way. And wasn't that what he'd been doing for most of his life, anyway?

He glanced at the security system coding. It was not specific to James' home—this Omni-Forge company ran the security systems of most of the residences in the area, and they all drew from the same source code. One of those phantom plans solidified a bit, granting him a sense of its shape. But before he could further contemplate it, something changed in James Clayton's home.

The coffee maker switched on.

Arcanthus clenched his jaw. A storm roiled just beneath the surface of his mind, crackling with lightning, rumbling with thunder, roaring with violent winds. Somehow, he kept it contained.

Though he felt Tenthil's eyes upon him, Arc didn't look away from the house and the holo screens. His own pent-up emotions roiled in the air, making the silence tense, tight, electric.

James Clayton resided there, in that large, private home, a home brimming with luxuries, while Samantha had been forced to live in a cramped apartment in an overcrowded building with neighbors who had looked at her like a piece of meat. She'd not had a single luxury but for the bitter tea she'd brought with her from Earth.

Arc had never been so naïve as to believe the universe was fair or just, but this...this was simply too much. Because despite her determination, despite her compassion, despite her inner strength, Samantha might well have never beaten the odds. She could've easily remained just another immigrant lost in Arthos, unfathomably far from her home, struggling to assemble some pathetic semblance of a life while the Infinite City held her down and kicked her.

Yet one of the amazing things about her, one of the things he loved, was that she would've found contentment in that. Somehow, she would have found contentment.

And James would've continued living his life of wealth and leisure, obtaining whatever he wanted—including Samantha—

by placing the appropriate number of credits in the right hands.

How had it taken Arcanthus so long to realize that he'd served as a pair of helping hands to people like James Clayton for years? He'd allowed himself to become a part of the very system he so railed against.

But none of this was about ethics or morals. He hadn't journeyed all the way to Earth to stop someone from trafficking a terran.

No, this was wholly personal.

When a sleek red hovercar approached the home a few minutes later, Arcanthus's heart quickened, and the raging maelstrom at his center swelled, pushing against its tenuous cage.

He watched the vehicle descend to the paved road and enter James's property through the front gate, watched it pass beneath the boughs of tall trees as it moved down the driveway, watched it finally reach the house.

As the vehicle came to a stop, Arc braced both hands on the dashboard and sat forward. The thumping of his heart became the only sound in the world. The car door opened, and a male human climbed out.

Everything within Arcanthus stilled and fell quiet, even that storm.

The terran was tall, with a lean, athletic build accentuated by his dark suit. His golden-brown hair was combed back, though it had been slightly tousled. Arcanthus had hated Vaund, who'd betrayed Arc, killed his friends, and hacked off his limbs, but that hatred had not truly blossomed until the bastard had threatened Samantha.

Arc's feelings toward Vaund were nothing compared to this.

Looking upon James Clayton for the first time in person,

Arcanthus felt a hatred so vast, so hot, so consuming, that it could've swallowed entire galaxies. He could not see James without imagining everything the man must've made Samantha suffer. The insults, the violations, the beatings, the lies and manipulation. She'd offered few details on most of it, and Arc had never wanted to press her, but it was all terribly clear to him in that moment.

Arcanthus's cybernetic limbs nearly trembled with rage, and his tail curled around his leg, squeezing tightly enough to hurt itself. He ground his teeth together as his *qal* scorched his flesh like fiery brands.

James closed the hovercar door, climbed the steps, and entered his home.

"Sedhi..." Tenthil rasped.

The zenturi's voice came to Arcanthus as though from an alternate, overlapping reality. He could not remove his gaze from the front door of the house; he didn't trust himself to move any part of his body so much as a millimeter. Because any movement, however miniscule, would've carried him out of the vehicle and straight to that door.

"Sedhi, *think*," said Tenthil. "Now is not the time."

"Now is the only time," Arcanthus growled, finally tearing his eyes away from the house.

My way. My time. No one else's. Because she is mine. Mine to love, mine to protect.

His fingers set into motion before his mind understood what he was doing. The plan had finally formed, and it would go into effect *now*. He altered and removed sections of coding in the Omni-Forge file, letting instinct guide him. With his other hand, he brought up the system for the local power company.

Again, Tenthil's heavy, scrutinous gaze was upon Arcanthus. "Do you even understand any of that?"

"Enough of it. I have a task for you," Arcanthus said as he pulled up a holographic map of the local power infrastructure.

A growl tore from Tenthil's chest. "Told you I'm not getting any more involved."

"I need you to go here"—Arc indicated a location in the model, which he overlaid on a map of the neighborhood—"and disable the substation."

"You're not fucking listening."

"You can hide yourself from surveillance. I cannot, at least not without rousing suspicions." Arcanthus met Tenthil's gaze. "Do this for me, zenturi, and I'll have all the rest done within an hour."

As the two held that eye contact, Arc's heart quickened further. Even if Tenthil refused, Arcanthus would find a way. He would take any risk to keep his mate safe. Would do anything to avenge her suffering.

Clarity descended upon Arc; he understood suddenly what Tenthil risked by his mere presence here. His family. Arc risked the same. But inaction would have worse consequences than this, and no threat to himself was too great to make him ignore a threat to Samantha. All his hatred and fury focused down to a single point—to an unshakeable determination.

"You owe me nothing, Tenthil," Arcanthus said, voice low, "but I ask you all the same."

Tenthil's lips peeled back, baring those double fangs, and his pupils expanded. "Fuck," he snarled. "Anything goes wrong, Arc, and I will not hesitate to leave you."

Arcanthus smiled, though it felt more like he was baring his own fangs. "I'd expect nothing less, my friend.

As he opened the cab door, Tenthil snapped, "Not friends."

Arc leaned closer. "You haven't killed me yet. If that's not friendship, I don't know what is."

Tenthil slammed the door in his face and stormed off.

FOURTEEN

James Clayton's home was not like Arcanthus had expected. He'd seen almost every part of it through the security system, but that wasn't the same as physically being in a place. It was never the same as standing in an environment with objects all around to be touched and examined; it was never the same as feeling the energy in the air.

This house was cold and dark, and Arc doubted that would change even after the power was restored.

As Arcanthus stalked along the hallway, checking the silent rooms—some of which were dark enough for his *qal*'s glow to spread several meters beyond their thresholds—he slowly built a broader understanding of the owner. In this case, that was the result more of what wasn't on display than what was.

The furniture, décor, and arrangement of every room was exemplary of comfortable wealth utterly lacking in personality. Every choice was oddly safe, oddly generic, which did not escape Arc's notice despite his limited knowledge of Earth fashions and traditions.

Tenthil and Abella's small apartment had held more character than existed in this entire house.

There were no images of family or friends, no hints at any hobbies or personal interests, nothing about James at all. Everything was excessively neat and clean. It was clear, even in the poor lighting, that not so much as a speck of dust lay where James didn't want it.

This didn't feel like a lived-in place.

Control. It's always about control.

James Clayton was not downstairs, but the coffee maker had already been drained and cleaned.

Even with the intensity of his rage and hatred, Arc maintained his focus and outward calm. He didn't hurry his step, didn't lash his tail, didn't submit to his urges to smash furniture, break windows, and punch holes in the walls. All his strength and capacity for violence would have but one target today.

He walked up the stairs, unconcerned with the soft creaks and groans they made beneath his weight. Part of Arcanthus wanted James to know that he was not alone, to feel panic, to experience burgeoning terror.

The second-floor hallway was even darker than its ground-level counterpart; all the doors were closed but for one at the end of the hall, which led to the master bedroom. It was cracked enough for Arcanthus to make out the gray evening light streaming in through the tinted windows.

A faint sound drifted to Arcanthus—running water.

His heart thumped, and anger nearly seized his limbs and froze him in place. He forced himself onward and didn't hesitate to push the door open completely when he reached it.

While the rest of the house suggested James was fond of gray and beige, this bedroom was dominated by dark, moody colors. Maroon and black on the bedding, deep blue and purple on the carpet, a red-purple accent wall. They were some of the same colors Arcanthus preferred, but here, they lacked the sensuality he normally associated with them.

Here, they were somehow oppressive and bleak.

Arcanthus crossed the room and halted at the bathroom door. Surely enough, the shower was running on the other side.

Clenching his jaw, Arcanthus moved away and performed a quick search of the room. There was little of note save for the loaded blaster pistol in the nightstand drawer. He picked the weapon up, examined it, and returned it to its place minus its power cell. The extra power cells buried deeper in the drawer did not concern him.

"You must have something," Arcanthus muttered, turning his head to scan the room. "People like you always do."

Because people like James Clayton rarely faced consequences for anything. Many thought themselves above the system, too rich, influential, and intelligent to get caught. And James seemed to believe that even before his recent inheritance of his father's fortune.

His eyes stopped on an opening on the far side of the room. It was only open a crack, like the bedroom entrance had been, but what stood out about this door was that it didn't appear to be a door at all—it looked like another piece of the wall. He didn't recall seeing anything indicating a room there in house's floorplans, and there'd certainly been no camera covering such a space.

Arcanthus approached the opening, and as he neared, the weak, flickering light from within grew apparent. Something sank in his gut as he placed his hand upon the door.

He hesitated. A smell emanated from beyond the opening, only just detectable, one he'd never picked up before, yet which was oddly familiar. A terran smell. A sex smell. But it wasn't at all like Samantha's alluring fragrance.

Barely suppressing a growl, he pushed the door open.

The source of the glow immediately caught his attention. One of the walls was recessed, with shelving built into it. Those shelves were filled with tiny holo projectors, all powered on and displaying images of female terrans—many of them undressed, many with James. Several of them appeared in multiple holos, but one female was in more than half of them. A female Arc recognized instantly.

His heart constricted and ceased beating. Everything within him went taut, his veins burned, and his lungs refused to fill with air.

Samantha.

My Samantha.

She was in so many of those holograms. Sometimes alone, sometimes with James, and in a few, with James and one or more other females. A great deal of her bare body was on display in many of the images.

Machinery buzzed in Arcanthus's limbs as they flexed involuntarily, placing new strain upon the body to which they were attached.

Somehow, he coaxed himself into motion and entered the room. He felt so much at once that he couldn't feel anything at all; all those emotions had smashed together into an indecipherable mass lodged deep in his chest.

A few of those holos showed a Samantha who was happy. A Samantha who had lost her support system after her father's death but mistakenly believed she'd met a male who would love her, cherish her, and respect her. Those were the most innocent of the images, and the only ones she'd likely taken willingly. All the rest...

He didn't want to look at any of the holos. Didn't want to see his mate like that, didn't want to see her with *him*. And though Arcanthus had made love to her so many, many times, though he'd explored, learned, and worshipped every millimeter of her gorgeous body, this was wrong. This was a violation. He knew Samantha well enough to know that she hadn't consented to this—not to the holos being recorded, not to them being displayed, not to the situations they depicted.

Arcanthus saw his mate with tears in her eyes, with bruises on her pale skin, with fear and confusion and sorrow etched upon her features. He saw her with James's hands on her body, with him inside her, saw the pain on her face. He saw James hitting her, tearing her clothing, restraining and choking her.

And he saw the malicious pleasure on James's face through all of it.

Arcanthus bared his gritted teeth.

The reality was so much worse than he had imagined, so much worse than he ever wanted to imagine. And it was all exacerbated by the fact that several of the holos were set on video loops, granting the images obscene motion.

Eventually, Arc managed to pry his eyes away from the display to study the rest of the room. His heartbeat thundered in his ears, broken only by his increasingly ragged breaths.

A bench seat with leather upholstery had been built into the wall on the right, facing the opposite wall, where heavy metal rings were mounted—the sort to which one might have connected restraints or chains.

Grasping one of the rings, Arc gave it a tug. It remained firmly in place. He exhaled heavily through his nostrils.

The overhead lights flickered on, and a male terran directly behind Arcanthus said, "Down."

Arc swung his tail hard, but it didn't connect with his assailant. He used the momentum to spin himself around, throwing a powerful cross punch. But his eyes widened when he realized what he was seeing.

He knew that shapely little body, he knew that brown hair, he knew that self-conscious stance, meant to make a small female seem smaller still. It wasn't James behind him, it was Samantha.

And it was too late to halt the savage blow.

He disrupted his own balance in a panic. His fist passed into Samantha's neck and out through her shoulder, and Arcanthus was falling, unable to reconcile what he was seeing with what he was feeling, what he was thinking.

His whole body passed through Samantha as he tumbled to the floor. He scrambled onto his back and shoved away from her, only to be halted by the bench seat.

Arcanthus lifted his gaze.

Samantha stood naked before him, with her face angled down and her arms covering her breasts and pelvis. Her skin was red. He knew his mate, knew that color was not due to the heat of arousal but of embarrassment, of shame.

"Down," the male voice repeated in a snarl.

Samantha flinched and turned away as though to shield herself. Voice weaker than Arcanthus had ever heard, she said, "Please. I-I don't like this."

Tears welled in those big brown eyes. Arcanthus's heart cracked.

"What did you say?" the male demanded.

"I don't like this, James." Samantha's tongue slipped out to run across her dry lips. "Please, c-can we stop?"

She cried out and stumbled backward. James was suddenly there. His hand darted out and caught her by the throat, choking off her cry. She grabbed his arm with both hands as he dragged her closer, her resistance amounting to nothing.

James leaned down as he forced her face up toward his. With his free hand, he unbuckled his belt and opened his pants. "How many fucking times do I have to tell you, Sam? When I give you a command, you obey it. You belong to me. When I want, where I want, whatever the fuck I want, you give it."

He pulled out his erect cock and brought his mouth to her ear. "You exist solely for my pleasure, my love."

But all you can have is my voice. My command.
Not him.

Rage quaked through Arcanthus, rapidly building into something so immense and powerful that he barely felt it. The pounding of his heart, deep, fast, and steady, resonated through his body, right down to his bones.

Command. That had been the word that triggered Samantha's panic while she and Arc were on their holo call. That had been the wound he'd unknowingly opened, the trauma he'd roused.

Something creaked; he did not immediately realize that it had been his jaw, clamped so tightly shut that his bones ached. Carpet fibers tore beneath his clawing fingers.

He knew what this room was, knew what it had been used for, what James Clayton intended to use it for. The ringed brackets on the wall were not decorative, the cushioned seat was not for relaxation, and the many holo projectors were not meant to preserve cherished memories of past relationships.

This was a trophy room, where a terrible person came to indulge in his obsessions.

And Samantha Dawn Wilder remained foremost of those obsessions.

Barely resisting the urge to attack what he knew to be a hologram, Arcanthus shoved himself to his feet. The normally smooth, languid movements of his body were stiff, and his tail thrashed behind him with violent, jerky motions. The doorframe splintered in his hand when he grasped it to pull himself through.

His gaze snapped to the bathroom door, which swung open after a click of the latch.

FIFTEEN

James Clayton emerged from the bathroom dressed only in a pair of undershorts, his attention focused on the holocom he was fastening to his wrist. "Fucking power company."

In his mind's eye, Arcanthus saw himself charge across the room, grab James by the hair, and slam the terran's face into the wall. He saw James fall, saw himself driving his knee into the man's head repeatedly, and he heard bone crunching and blood gushing. His imagination flooded with a crimson tide.

Yet Arc allowed himself only a single step forward and—voice impossibly calm and steady—said, "Their repairs seemed rather expeditious to me."

The terran started, halting partway between the door and the bed, eyes rounded in startlement. "What the fuck?"

Arcanthus slowly unbuttoned his suit jacket as he walked along the wall opposite the human. "Forgive me, James. The doorbell wasn't working, so I let myself in."

The terran's initial surprise had been replaced by an all-too-familiar gleam in his eyes—a sort of malevolent smugness that was common back in the Undercity. It was the look of a person who was convinced he'd already won. A person who'd rarely, if ever, had to struggle for anything in his life.

Eyebrows slanting down, James turned his body toward Arcanthus. "Forge, there's an intruder."

Arcanthus paused and turned to face the man, tilting his head to the side.

James's smugness cracked when he received no reply from either his security system or Arc. He glanced up. "Forge! Intruder! Activate home defense procedures."

Chuckling, Arcanthus took off his jacket and resumed his leisurely walk. Every part of his body growled in protest of his inaction. "I'm afraid that your security system is experiencing technical difficulties at the moment."

Nostrils flaring, James glared at Arcanthus. "Who the fuck are you?"

Arc folded the jacket over his arm and tossed it onto the dresser before unfastening the cuffs of his shirt. "Normally, I would choose from a number of potential answers to that question, but none of those would mean anything to you." He rolled up a sleeve, carefully folding the fabric.

With a growl, James strode to the nightstand, yanked open the drawer, and drew the blaster pistol from within. He aimed the weapon at Arcanthus. "Shut your fucking mouth. No more talking."

Arcanthus's tail swept across the carpet and thumped the wall behind him. "I assure you, James"—he began rolling up his other sleeve—"you do not want to skip the talking part."

James held the blaster higher. "Initiate call. Local police."

His holocom came on, bringing up a small holo screen for the call. Arcanthus couldn't read most of the terran letters it displayed, especially not reversed, but he recognized the no connection icon.

Growling again, James retried the call. The result was the same.

Arc stepped toward the terran, heart quickening in anticipation. So close now. So close to the end of this.

"Back up!" James extended his arm fully, lining up the weapon's barrel with Arc's third eye. "I will shoot you."

"You would, wouldn't you?" Arcanthus advanced another pace. "But if you did, we'd lose our opportunity to discuss your business on Arthos, wouldn't we?"

Surprise flickered across James's face, but he hastily regained his composure. "I don't know wh—"

"You sent bounty hunters after a female terran who immigrated to Arthos." Frowning, Arcanthus smoothed a wrinkle on his rolled-up sleeve. He wasn't sure how he was maintaining such self-control, but he was glad for it; he wanted James to know exactly what all this was about.

"You people were supposed to communicate only through indirect channels, God damn it." James lowered the blaster. "What the fuck are you doing here? Did you find her?"

"I did." Arcanthus dropped his hands into his pockets. Electric currents raced along his prostheses and just beneath his skin. He couldn't tell whether they originated in his flesh and blood parts or his machine parts.

"You were supposed to hand her off to my people on Arthos, not show up at my damned house."

Arcanthus snickered and shook his head. "James, you misunderstand."

"Misunderstand?" The terran stepped closer, the angry light in his eyes flaring. How many times had Samantha seen that light? How many times had it pierced her heart with dread?

How many times had she wondered whether she'd survive to the next day?

James jabbed a finger toward Arc. "The deal was set, the arrangements made. Find her, catch her, and hand her off. That was all. So if you think you're going to coax even a single credit out of me above what we agreed upon, you're sorely mistaken."

Though James was at least ten centimeters shorter than Arcanthus, that still left him significantly taller than Samantha—certainly large enough for her to have had little hope of defending herself against his aggression, even if she'd had some of the training she'd received while living with Arcanthus.

Arc closed the distance between himself and the terran with a single stride, bumping his chest into James's finger. "I don't work for you, James."

The terran snapped his hand away and retreated a step. "So what, is this a shakedown or something? Think I'll pay more just because I want her?"

Despite his best efforts, Arcanthus couldn't keep a growl out of his next words, which made his stomach twist into a knot. "Well, you do believe she belongs to you, don't you?"

James backed up farther and aimed the blaster at Arcanthus again. "What is this? Who are you?"

"She is under my protection now."

"Protection?" The terran scoffed. "Whatever she's paying you, I'll give you ten times as much just to tell me where she is. Twenty if you bring her here."

Arcanthus kept pace with the human's retreat. His body thrummed with fury begging for release, and the pressure in his chest was so great that it threatened to crush his insides. "I have no interest in money, only in the love she has given me. A concept you would not understand, as the only love you have is for yourself."

"Love?" James spat. Anger battled the fear and uncertainty in his eyes. "Love? I gave her nothing but love, but she ran from me to fuck *you?*" Releasing a bestial snarl, he pulled the blaster's trigger over and over again.

The weapon produced a series of soft clicks.

James's eyes rounded and darted up to meet Arcanthus's. He squeezed the trigger again, and again the blaster did not fire.

Arcanthus plucked the power cell from his pocket and held it up between forefinger and thumb. "They don't tend to do much without one of these, James."

The terran spun around and hurried to the nightstand, tearing the drawer off its tracks and spilling its contents across the carpet. With a curse, he dropped to his knees and clawed through the mess.

Soon, Samantha. All this will be done soon.

Arc advanced on his prey.

Laughter, equal parts panicked, spiteful, and triumphant, bubbled from James's throat as he snatched a spare power cell from the debris. He reared back on his knees and flicked open the blaster's power cell compartment.

"So close, James." Arcanthus clamped a hand around the blaster and tugged on it.

The terran swayed, and the fresh cell fell from his fumbling hands.

Arcanthus squeezed. The blaster groaned as it bent and warped, unable to withstand the strength of his cybernetic prosthesis. A twist of his wrist tore the ruined weapon from the terran's hold.

"Fuck," James rasped, flinging himself away from Arcanthus. He rushed to the bed and scrambled across it, disrupting the neat bedding as he bounced and flailed.

"What's wrong, James?" Arcanthus reached the bed just as his quarry came down on the other side. "Don't you want to hit me?" Thrusting a hand under the mattress, he flipped the entire thing off its frame; it landed partly atop the terran, knocking him to the floor and tangling him in the bedding.

The terran thrashed to free himself, tumbling over and off the mattress with the blanket twisted around his legs. "Just get the fuck out of here! Keep the fuck away from me!"

Arcanthus continued his steady pursuit as James stumblingly regained his feet. "Not until all this is settled."

"I'll call them off!" James spun toward Ac, nearly tripping over his own legs in the process, and raised his hands placatingly. "I'll leave her alone."

"We both know it's much too late for that, James."

The terran backed up until he bumped into the wall. His breathing was quick and ragged, and a sheen of sweat glistened on his skin. "I don't know what she told you, but she lied. She's fucking lying."

Arcanthus again closed the distance between himself and James and backhanded the terran across the face. James's head snapped aside, and he staggered in the same direction. Before the man could fall, Arcanthus grabbed a fistful of his hair and yanked him upright.

The human's eyes rolled before focusing on Arcanthus. One side of his face was bright red, and a drop of crimson had welled on his lip where his skin had split.

"You don't get to speak about her ever again," Arcanthus said.

James wiped his mouth with the back of his hand, glancing briefly at the blood smeared on his skin. "Who the fuck do you think you are?"

"Clearly wealth cannot buy intelligence."

Snarling, James grabbed Arcanthus's wrist and pulled up on it. "You have no idea how fucking dead you are."

Arc's arm didn't budge, and he did not loosen his grip on the terran's hair. "What are you going to do? Are you going to fight, or just make hollow threats? Perhaps you'd like to call the police commissioner directly?"

"You don't scare me, you three-eyed freak. I have resources. Men, power, credits. You'll be hunted down like the beast you are." James gave another fierce tug on Arc's arm, and again failed to move it. "Let go. Now."

"You have a lot to answer for, James." Arcanthus leaned closer. "And you will answer for all of it. Every last bit."

Terror glinted in the human's eyes. "You're making a mistake."

Chuckling, Arcanthus patted James's reddened cheek, making him flinch. "All the mistakes have been yours, and there are so, so many of them. I do have one regret, however. I should have paid you a visit months ago. It would've saved us both some trouble."

"We can work out a deal," James said hurriedly, nodding to himself. "Yeah. Everyone wants something, right? What do you want? Drugs? Sex? I hear human women are pretty popular out in space. Maybe you want a few more of your own?"

"I'm not surprised that understanding continues to elude you. Allow me to offer as clear an answer as possible." Arcanthus tugged James's head away from the wall and slammed it back. The material cracked and buckled inward.

James let out a pained cry. His legs wobbled, and briefly, Arc's hold on his hair was the only thing keeping the terran upright.

"No, no," Arcanthus rumbled, patting James's face again. "You don't get to escape this. Not a single fucking moment. Just like you didn't allow her any escape."

"That's why she's on fucking Arthos?" the terran growled through his teeth. "That ungrateful bi—"

Arc hammered a fist into the human's gut, doubling him over and cutting off those words. When James began to sag with a wheeze, Arcanthus hauled him up even higher by the hair. "You don't seem to learn, do you? What did I tell you?"

James's nostrils flared with his heavy, panting breaths as he struggled to get his feet planted on the floor. His lips peeled back, and spittle flew out through his gritted teeth. He adjusted his hold on Arcanthus's arm to support himself.

Though the questions had been rhetorical, Arcanthus couldn't keep his anger from intensifying at the terran's lack of a response. But there was a fire in James's eyes, burning just behind the pain and fear; hatred and fury of his own.

Releasing the terran's hair, Arcanthus took a step back and dropped his hands into his pockets. His heart was like endlessly rolling thunder in his chest, and heat radiated from it in waves. Whatever had allowed him to contain his rage would not last much longer, but he wasn't ready to lose control. Not yet.

"All the times you hurt her, James...did you ever hesitate? Did you ever question yourself? Did you even once feel fear for the consequences?"

The terran flattened a hand against the wall to steady himself. "Fuck you."

Arcanthus grinned. "Of course you didn't fear the consequences. You were confident that there wouldn't be any, because you come from wealth and influence. You've never had to fight for anything. You've never known struggle. Not that it would have made a difference, because your deficiencies run straight to your soul. All along, you've been a coward and a weakling, and you target people like her to make yourself feel strong."

James scowled and stood a little taller. Fresh blood trickled down his chin from his split lip, and strands of his hair had fallen into his face, one side of which was an even deeper red than before.

"Come, James," Arcanthus said, dipping his chin toward

the terran. "Strike me. Show me your strength. Show me your fury."

The human again wiped blood away from his mouth. When he lowered his arm, he curled his hands into fists, but he didn't make another move.

Fire blazed in Arcanthus's gut, scorching a path through his chest and up into his throat. It was fueled by all the pain and suffering Samantha had endured, which he could soothe but never take away, by all the memories haunting her that he could distract her from but never fully erase, by all the sorrow and torment of not being able to care for his mate in every way she could possibly need. Those flames roared higher and higher.

Arcanthus stepped closer, now chest-to-chest with James, and angled his face down to hold the terran's gaze. "Would it help if you imagine I'm her? Is that what it will take?"

"I never hurt her," James grated. "She exaggerates. Makes shit up. I gave her the whole fucking world, treated her like a queen."

"Oh?" Arcanthus gestured over his shoulder. "So I suppose all the images in your little secret room are fabricated, correct? Or is it terran custom to assault your queen?"

The terran blanched, and his throat bobbed as he swallowed. "Don't know what the hell you're talking about. I always treated her right."

"You treated her like property. Like a toy. You kept her prisoner."

"I kept her in her fucking place!" James planted his hands on Arc's chest and shoved hard.

Twisting aside, Arcanthus grasped the terran's wrists and used James's force to throw him. The human's feet left the floor, and his momentum carried him into a flip that saw him crashing down on his back and skidding along the carpet. Arcanthus was there before the terran could get up, taking a fistful of that golden brown hair and pulling James's head off the floor.

"Time to put you in your place," Arc snarled.

The terran grunted and threw a wild punch. Arcanthus caught the man's fist in the palm of his hand and closed his fingers around it.

"Did you picture her? Did you imagine your fist"—Arc squeezed, coaxing a pained growl from James—"striking her face?" Wrenching the terran's head back, Arcanthus knelt and leaned very close. "Because I have. Every day since she told me about you."

Bone crunched in James's hand as Arcanthus increased the pressure. Both that sound and the agonized scream that escaped the human's throat heightened Arc's need to spill blood, to inflict pain, to destroy this male one piece at a time.

"You will never hurt her again." Arcanthus released James's mangled hand and rose, hauling the terran up with him.

James clutched his hand against his belly, eyes watering, pained cries continuing.

"What's wrong, James?" Arcanthus asked. "Does it hurt?"

"You fucking broke my hand," the terran cried. "*Fuck.* What the fuck? What the fuck."

"Breathe through it." Arc dragged the terran toward the secret room.

"Please, stop. God." James groaned, scrambling to get his feet planted on the carpet to no avail. "No more. No fucking more. You're...you're fucking me up."

Arcanthus laughed humorlessly. "Did you think I traveled all this way just to have a friendly chat, James?"

"Please," the terran repeated.

With a roar, Arcanthus flung James forward. The human hit the door hard enough to snap it partly off the frame and splinter the wood, landing in a heap against the shelving wall.

The holo projectors rattled, some of them flickering and falling over.

The life-sized hologram of Samantha and James was still active at the center of the room, where Sam, with tears streaming down her cheeks, was now on her knees before the man.

"Did you relent when she pleaded with you?" Arcanthus stalked into the room as James pawed at the shelves, further disturbing the projectors, in an attempt to pull himself to his feet.

Arcanthus kicked James's flailing arm, producing a satisfying snap and drawing another scream from him. The terran fell, shoulder and face taking the brunt of the impact against the wall.

Again taking the human by the hair, Arcanthus dragged him around and slammed his back against the wall. James stared up with wide, wild, fearful eyes, so terribly different from the smug, spiteful gaze of only minutes before.

"Did you show her mercy?" Arc demanded.

"Please," James rasped.

Arcanthus hammered the terran's head back, putting a dent in the wall. James's eyes rolled, going nearly all white, and his body sagged. Growling, Arcanthus tugged sharply up on the man's hair. James's eyes flared.

"I told you, James. You don't get an easy escape." Arcanthus crouched, putting his face closer to level with the terran's. "You will feel every bit of this, and even that will be but a fraction of what you deserve. Did. You. Relent?"

Lower lip trembling, James shook his head.

Arcanthus slapped the terran across the other cheek, immediately forcing the man to face him again. "Why?"

Those rounded eyes, now bloodshot and glistening, swept

rapidly from side to side as though the answer were hidden somewhere on Arc's face.

Holographic James groaned in pleasure and muttered, "You nick me with your teeth this time and I swear I'm going to knock them out."

Jaw clenched, Arcanthus stared down at the terran. His rage swelled, reaching new strength, even as the terror on James's face deepened.

"No," James said. "No, I didn't mean—"

Arcanthus's fist silenced James Clayton. Blood sprayed from the terran's mouth and spattered the wall and carpet, and at least two crimson-stained teeth accompanied it.

Flesh James groaned, but not in pleasure—the sound was a curse, a plea, a prayer. He coughed, and fresh blood and spit bubbled from his smashed lips. Words mangled, he asked, "For her? All this...for her?"

"I would do anything for her," Arcanthus snarled. "To protect her. To avenge her. To love her. *Anything.*"

"Never again. Wont...t-talk to her. L-look for her." James shook his head, though he barely managed to move it at all. "Never."

Arcanthus bared his teeth. "Never."

He stood up, again hauling James with him, though the terran didn't support himself this time.

James's wheezing breaths passed through his ruined teeth, ejecting fresh blood and saliva. "All this...for Saman—"

Arcanthus's free hand clamped around the terran's throat, cutting off those words. Arc lifted the man off the ground and slammed him against the wall, ratting the projectors on the shelves. "You will never again speak her name." His grip tightened. "You will never again so much as *think* her name."

James writhed, heels repeatedly thumping the wall, but he kept his wounded arms tucked against his torso. His face rapidly darkened, shifting from red toward purple. His eyes bulged.

When Arcanthus eased his grip to ensure the terran didn't prematurely lose consciousness, James choked out a question.

"What're you going to do to me?"

"Fucking faster, damn it," holographic James snapped, prompting a distressed, muffled cry from holographic Samantha.

Arcanthus's tail slammed on the floor, and his lips stretched into a wide, bloodthirsty grin. "Take my time, James. I'm going to take my fucking time."

SIXTEEN

Large, sporadic raindrops were pelting the hovercar when the sedhi returned. Tenthil watched as Arcanthus opened the passenger door and climbed in.

Though Arc's attire appeared as neatly put together and expensive as before, a blood scent clung to him, and Tenthil spotted a few dark stains on the fabric of his pants. The sedhi's hair, swept back over one shoulder, looked as though it had been recently combed. But the light in Arcanthus's eyes was the true difference.

Before, it had been a blinding flame, blazing with fury. Now it was a smoldering ember, fading but not yet extinguished.

Without a word, Tenthil engaged the antigrav drives and began the journey back to California. Arcanthus folded his arms across his chest and leaned his shoulder against the door, staring out the window.

Fifteen minutes passed, leaving Seattle far behind, and Arcanthus remained quiet. Tenthil had yet to sort out his feelings regarding silence. Having been raised in the Order of the

Void, he'd thought silence was natural, something in which to find comfort. Yet he'd grown to resent it.

Silence was *not* natural. Life meant noise, sometimes so much of it that one could not think straight, and though it was common for that noise to be broken by quiet lulls, these long, lingering silences were troubling.

It was particularly unsettling coming from someone like Arcanthus, who'd seemed incapable of shutting his mouth for more than a few seconds at a time.

Tenthil switched to autopilot and looked at the sedhi. "What's wrong?"

Arcanthus frowned. "Nothing is wrong."

"Too quiet."

"Yes, you typically are."

"Not me."

"I'm thinking."

Tenthil narrowed his eyes. "You are brooding."

Arcanthus turned his face toward Tenthil, brow knitted. "For someone who has worked so hard to erect boundaries between us, zenturi, you are certainly testing them now."

Tenthil barely held back a chuckle—it was astonishing that the sound had even threatened to come from him to begin with, given all that had happened. "Just stating fact, sedhi."

"Your interpretation of an observation is not, by default, a fact."

"It is when it's right."

"I am *not* brooding." When Tenthil only stared at him, Arc continued, "So what if I am a touch sensitive? It's normal. Most people experience emotions."

Tenthil's eyebrows fell. "I have emotions."

Arc snickered and shook his head. "Emotions apart from anger and murder."

Growling, Tenthil turned his torso toward the sedhi. "Murder is not an emotion."

"Isn't it? You have met yourself, haven't you, Tenthil?"

"Sedhi..."

Arcanthus returned his attention to the passenger window, his expression suddenly solemn. "Your mate was taken. No details, I know, and I don't need any to know you spilled a sea of blood to get her back. And when that was done, when the last threat to her lay vanquished...how did it feel?" Arc met Tenthil's gaze then. Something had replaced the ember of fury in the sedhi's eyes—a burgeoning vulnerability.

Letting out a slow, heavy breath, Tenthil faced forward. In many ways, that time of his life had been the most confusing and troubling. What wounds he'd suffered on his soul were still healing. Yet one thing had been clear throughout that time, one thing had been certain.

Abella.

And he would never forget his fear, his rage, his love, his ultimate relief, would never forget his enduring worry.

"Felt...lighter," Tenthil said, battling an intensifying burn in his throat. "Felt...right. But even with them dead on the floor and her in my arms, part of me couldn't believe it was over. That she was safe, and we were free."

Arcanthus nodded, drumming his fingers on his bicep. "Yes, that sounds about right."

Tenthil found himself studying the sedhi, again seeing him in a new light. "But it is done, Arc. You finished it."

"I did. And the evidence he left behind will show this world who and what he was, show them the wrongs he committed, though they'll never know my mate was part of it. She will not be tainted by this. He has no further power over her." A smirk crept onto Arc's face. "And it pleases me to know he would be furious regarding the fate of his fortune."

Tenthil arched a brow.

"No, zenturi, I didn't take it. His will clearly dictates that all his assets are to be sold off, with the proceeds—along with his substantial savings and investments—to be donated to various domestic abuse charities and women's shelters. They'll put it to better use than I ever could. And to ensure that the gesture is not misconstrued, the language specifies that he took this step out of guilt for his wrongdoings."

"Death wasn't enough?" Before Tenthil had even finished asking the question, he recalled the Master, and he knew the answer.

Arcanthus unfolded his arms and stared down at his palms. "Not one death. Not ten deaths, or a hundred, or a thousand. But however much I want to kill him again, that's not possible. So I'll take what I can get."

Despite himself, a smile twitched into place on Tenthil's lips. "Sounds about right."

Arcanthus grinned and fell silent again, but Tenthil no longer found it uncomfortable. He understood. He sympathized. And, more than anything, he couldn't wait to have his mate in his arms again, so he could tell her—and show her—just how much he loved her.

SEVENTEEN

Urgand and Sekk'thi were sitting on the couch when Arcanthus entered the suite, the lean ilthurii tucked against the stocky vorgal with a blanket draped over their bodies. Some old, two-dimensional human movie was on the main holo screen, its actors dressed in ancient looking costumes.

There was an odd scent in the air, apart from the lingering smell of terran food. It was pleasant, almost familiar, a sweetness that Arc should have been able to identify, but he had neither the energy nor the inclination to puzzle it out.

Arcanthus paused behind the couch, turning to watch the screen. Several people with wildly varying statures were seated together around a stone pedestal, atop which lay a golden ring. The pointed ears and thick facial hair on some of the actors did not disguise that they were humans.

He peeled off his suit jacket, looked down, and frowned at the bloodstains on his shirt. The clothing would need to be properly disposed of; even if terran authorities would never find Arcanthus back on Arthos, he didn't intend to leave even the faintest trail behind.

In the movie, a character with a bushy red beard attempted to destroy the ring with an axe, managing only to shatter his blade and knock himself onto his ass.

"Ah, yes," Arc said as he unbuttoned his shirt, "a good reminder that I need to check in with the jeweler tomorrow."

"Shut up," Urgand grumbled.

Arc scoffed, staring at the back of the vorgal's head. "That's the greeting I get?"

"Trying to watch this."

Wincing at the faint twinges in his tired muscles as he moved, Arcanthus tugged his shirt off. "Trying to watch a movie that has undoubtedly been charged to the person who rented the room?"

"So send me a fucking invoice, sedhi. Don't care as long as you shut up."

Sekk'thi's shoulders shook. It took Arcanthus a moment to realize that she was laughing.

"So, I've become a joke to the two of you?" Arc wadded up the soiled shirt.

"Become?" Urgand asked.

Sekk'thi turned her head, nostrils flaring with a deep inhalation. "Why do you smell of blood?"

Arcanthus raised the shirt. "I would imagine it's because I was covered in blood. Why do you smell like... Whatever that is?"

Urgand growled and paused the movie, slightly turning his head toward Arc. "You fucking did it alone."

"No, I did not do it alone," Arc replied, sweeping his hair back over his shoulder. "I had professional guidance."

Sekk'thi sat upright, tail thumping on the couch cushion, as Urgand flattened his palms on his thighs and pushed himself to his feet. The blanket fell away. The vorgal, who wasn't wearing so much as a scrap of clothing, slowly turned to face Arc, his features set in a scowl that would've made Drakkal proud.

The ilthurii wasn't wearing anything either, though she had decidedly fewer body parts that could dangle freely.

Arcanthus smirked, pointing from Urgand to Sekk'thi and back again. "Why are you both unclothed?"

"No." Urgand shook his head and leveled a finger at Arc. "You're not changing the fucking subject. What do you mean by professional guidance?"

"Do you recall the zenturi who came to get IDs for himself and his terran?"

Urgand pressed his hands over his face. "Arcanthus..."

"What is a zenturi?" asked Sekk'thi, cocking her head.

"An unintegrated species," Arcanthus said. "This one has pale gray skin, silver eyes, black claws." He traced a line from the corner of his mouth across his cheek with the tip of a finger. "Scars that make him look excessively happy all the time."

"The same zenturi who looked at most of us like he wanted to rip out our guts and strangle us with them?" asked Urgand. "The same zenturi who, according to Drakkal, was very nearly provoked into killing you, Arcanthus?"

Arcanthus frowned. "Yes, that one. But I will have you know that Drakkal's recollection of those events is highly suspect and tainted by his personal biases."

Running a hand back across her head scales, Sekk'thi asked, "You are saying Drakkal is biased against you? Are you two not close friends?"

"Very close. But he's never let go of the fact that I've defeated him every time we've faced each other in a serious contest."

The vorgal dragged his hands down, palms rasping across his face. His fingers snagged his lower lip, briefly pulling it down to display his short tusks in their entirety. "Could the two of you focus here, please?"

"The zenturi is a former assassin. It certainly made sense to consult him regarding this matter, did it not?" Arcanthus turned his palms up, spread his arms to the sides, and shrugged. "But the business is done, at any rate. Once I collect the ring, we..."

Arcanthus's words faded. Narrowing his eyes, he settled his hands on the back of the couch and leaned over it, staring at Urgand's face. "What happened to your lip, vorgal?"

Urgand's eyes rounded, and he eased back. "Don't know what you're talking about."

"I've seen more than my share of split lips, and yours is a prime example. What happened?"

"A fight. Nothing serious."

Arcanthus huffed. "A fight? All you had to do was lie low for a few days. Not go out and rough up the damned city!"

"Well, you fucking ran off again! Did you really think we were just going to sit on our asses and stare at the ceiling until you got back?"

"Yes!"

"Fuck that!"

"You were supposed to be safe."

"You're one to talk, *boss*."

"He took me to the ocean," said Sekk'thi in a gentle tone that served as the antithesis of Urgand and Arc's heated voices.

Something warmed in Arcanthus's chest, and his tension melted away. He wasn't angry with either of them, not really, but to say he wasn't brimming with lingering emotions from the day's events would've been a lie. Yet hearing Sekk'thi say that, recalling the way she and the vorgal had been sitting when Arcanthus arrived, that scent, their state of undress...

"Shit went bad for a few minutes," Urgand said, his voice

thick but much less aggressive. "Guess I stepped into the wrong part of town at the wrong time. But we salvaged the day."

Sekk'thi slid her tail up the back of Urgand's leg.

Arcanthus nodded. "I'm happy you two enjoyed yourselves despite me. And just know that it wasn't my intention to end this today, but...opportunity arose."

"We cannot blame you for seizing opportunity, can we?" Sekk'thi looked at Urgand. When he didn't say anything, she slapped the back of his thigh with her tail.

"Right," Urgand said hurriedly. "Can't blame you for that."

Arc smirked. "Well, I might've given said opportunity a bit of assistance in manifesting, but what's done is done." He pointed to the door of his bedroom. "I'm going to go clean up. I'll leave you two to...whatever this is."

"It is about a magical ring," Sekk'thi said, her eyes bright with excitement. "A ring that could destroy a whole world."

"Well, not the ring itself," Urgand amended. "And not really *destroy* as much as enslave. It's the one who made the ring, this dark lord who— Look, sedhi, you're welcome to watch with us, but we're not going to keep stopping to answer questions about the stuff you missed."

Slowly, Arcanthus looked from the vorgal to the ilthurii. His smirk softened, and he shook his head. "I wouldn't want to intrude. And, truly, I need a shower. You two enjoy." As he walked toward the bedroom, he added, "I would ask you to keep it down, but I know that would be terribly hypocritical of me."

He glanced over his shoulder.

Urgand's face darkened, but when he met Sekk'thi's gaze, he grinned, and heat sparked in their eyes.

Arcanthus slipped into the bedroom and closed the door behind him. He set the suit jacket and shirt aside, but he didn't immediately enter the washroom. Instead, he activated his holocom, and his fingers instinctively initiated a call.

Within moments, the holo projection came on, displaying Samantha's face. Her hair was mussed, her half-lidded eyes unfocused, and when she spoke, her voice was husky from sleep. "Arc? Is everything all right?"

Had there ever been a more beautiful sight, a more beautiful sound, in all existence? He smiled. "It is now."

She shifted, propping herself up on an elbow. She already seemed more alert. "Did something happen? Are you guys okay?"

"We are. Just a long, tiring day. But my business here is nearly concluded."

That he'd had to leave her to protect her was maddening, but she was safe now, and he'd endure this time apart a thousand times over if that was what it took to protect his mate.

His smile wavered. He could almost smell her alluring fragrance, could almost feel the warmth and softness of her skin against his, of her breath on his neck. "I've missed you, my flower."

EIGHTEEN

Samantha thrummed with anticipation. Staring at the closed garage door, she shifted her weight from one foot to the other and rubbed her thumbs along the hem of her sweater, which was clutched in her fists.

Arcanthus was coming home.

"Is he here yet?" she asked, and not for the first time. It wasn't even the second or third.

Drakkal let out a huff from just behind her. "Don't know. Want me to go check in the corners and behind the hovercars?"

Samantha peeked at him over her shoulder and smiled sweetly. "Maybe?"

His typical scowl lingered briefly before crumbling, and he shook his head. "Trust me when I say I'm just as eager for him to get here. Just for a different reason."

She turned and pointed at him. "There will be no wringing my mate's neck. Don't think I haven't heard you muttering under your breath while he's been gone."

"If I wring his neck, terran, it's only because I care."

"Maybe try giving him a hug?"

Drakkal folded his arms across his chest and planted his frown in place, albeit in an exaggeratedly grumpy fashion. "Oh, I'll give him a hug. Biggest hug he's ever had."

Samantha narrowed her eyes. "Promise you won't hurt him though?"

His forced smile bared his fangs in a way that wasn't exactly reassuring. "Promise."

Drakkal's holocom pinged.

Sam's breath hitched, and her eyes flicked to his cybernetic prosthesis—the one she'd designed for him after he'd lost his arm in the battle against Vaund. Her heart raced. "Is that him?"

He raised his arm and tapped the holocom built into its wrist. A small holo screen appeared, and Drakkal dismissed the message after glancing over it. "No. Just a reminder to myself to wring Arc's neck today."

Were Samantha a balloon, she would have deflated on the spot.

She turned back toward the garage door, crossed her arms over her chest, and worried on her bottom lip. These days without Arcanthus had felt like the longest of her life. Since the day he'd brought her to live at his compound—which had unfortunately been destroyed in the same attack that cost Drakkal his arm—Arcanthus had never left Sam. Even when they weren't side by side, he'd always been a short walk away, and knowing that she could've gone to see him any time had always been a comfort to her.

Not knowing where he was or if he was safe, being unable to see him or talk to him whenever she wanted, not having him randomly surprise her with a hug, a kiss, or a little gift while she was hyper focused on her art...it had been harder to endure than she'd imagined.

She just...*missed* him. Terribly. So much that it frightened her.

"Knowing him, Samantha, he's going to make a big, unannounced entrance right when—"

The garage door rose with a hum of unseen machinery. A black hovercar with tinted windows glided through the opening.

Sam's eyes widened.

He's here! He's here. He's finally back home.

She took a step toward the hovercar before she caught herself, forcing her feet to remain in place. Everything inside her demanded she race ahead.

Not yet, Sam! Let them at least park the car.

Before the car had even pulled into an open spot, the passenger door flew open. Samantha's heart skipped a beat as Arcanthus emerged from the still-moving vehicle, landing heavily but smoothly on his feet.

Inside the car, Urgand shouted, "What the fuck, Arc?"

Samantha barely heard the words.

With watery eyes and a huge smile, she ran toward Arcanthus, toward her mate, and he ran to meet her.

She leapt at Arc, throwing her arms and legs around him, and he caught her in a powerful embrace and buried his face against her neck, breathing in deep.

"My flower," he rasped, brushing his lips across her skin. One of his hands cupped the back of her head, fingers delving into her hair. "Fuck, but I've missed you."

Samantha squeezed her eyes shut and hugged him tighter. "I missed you too."

His sweet, woodsy scent, so reminiscent of sandalwood, enveloped her. She inhaled it. It was the same fragrance that haunted their bed, which had felt so large and empty for far too long. She'd hated waking up every morning only to be reminded that he was gone.

He grazed her neck with his nose and lips, sending a shiver through her.

She drew back, needing to see him, to kiss him, but she froze, heart clenching, when their eyes met. Not once in all the time she'd known him had she ever seen this strong male cry, and what she saw now undid her. Tears glistened in his eyes and traced paths down the gray skin of his cheeks, sparkling when they crossed his glowing *qal*.

"Arc..." She cupped his face and brushed away his tears with her thumbs. "What's wrong?"

Despite his tears, he smiled the most brilliant, charming smile. "Since I departed, I've felt incomplete. As though my soul had been shattered and I could not fit the pieces together. But now that I am with you, it's all clear, and I am made whole. I missed you, my strong, beautiful mate. I am not myself without you."

Tears stung her own eyes as she smiled and stroked her fingers through his hair, tucking the strands behind one of his long, pointed ears. "Everything is perfect now that you're home."

Cradling his jaw, she lowered her face and pressed her lips to his. At the first sweep of his tongue, she opened to him.

With a low growl, Arcanthus tightened his grip on her hair and slanted his head, deepening the kiss. His mouth and tongue wove a spell over her, equal parts caressing and claiming, spreading heat across her face and throughout her body. But the kiss also bespoke his need, showing her how much he'd missed her, craved her, *loved* her.

He held her as though he'd never let go.

Samantha slid her hands up and clasped his horns, kissing Arc with a ferocity to match his as she clenched her thighs around his sides. Whispers of pleasure flitted though her, and heat bloomed in her core. She wanted him now. It'd been so long since she'd felt his mouth on hers, felt his hands on her skin, felt his co—

Something heavy dropped to the ground, startling Sam. She broke the kiss, lifted her head, and looked at Urgand as he straightened behind Arc.

"Don't break anything," Arcanthus said with a hint of a growl, also turning his attention toward the vorgal.

"Don't jump out of moving vehicles," Urgand replied.

Arcanthus huffed. "Don't ruin the moment."

The heat blazing across Samantha's skin at that moment had nothing to do with passion. How had she forgotten that they had an audience?

"Oh, I've got a lot of *don'ts* to add if you want," Drakkal grumbled.

"No," Arc replied almost before Drakkal had finished speaking. He sighed and returned his attention to Samantha. "My apologies, my flower. It seems everyone I employ has a particular talent for interrupting at the most inopportune times."

Still feeling the warmth of embarrassment, Samantha smiled and brushed a finger over his bottom lip. "It's...probably good that he did."

After pecking a kiss on her finger, Arcanthus gently lowered Sam to her feet. "Perhaps. But they can only delay the inevitable." Fire blazed in his yellow eyes, which brimmed with promise Sam couldn't wait for him to fulfill. Even when he pulled away, she still felt the imprint of his touch on her body.

"I suppose this is as good a time as any, thanks to Urgand's express delivery." Arcanthus shot the vorgal a glare before crouching to pick up the plastic storage container Urgand had dropped. He turned to Sam, cradled the container on one cybernetic arm, and opened the lid. "For you."

Samantha glanced between the tote and Arcanthus. "You got me presents?"

He grinned. "Did you think I would leave and not return with gifts for my mate?"

That warmth flared upon her cheeks again. "Well, yes? I mean, you had business to worry about, which is usually the dangerous sort, and you had a lot on your mind, so it would—"

Arc caught her chin and tipped her face up, meeting her eyes. "My first and last thoughts, Samantha, are only of you."

Her chest constricted, and she again felt the sting of tears, but she held them back and smiled up at him.

How is it possible to love someone this much?

He stroked a finger along her jaw. "Now, take a look at what I have brought you from Earth."

Samantha blinked. It took her a moment to register what it was he had said. That...couldn't be right. Had he said... "Earth? You...you went to Earth?"

"I did. And one day, when you are ready to return, I long to go with you and see it through your eyes. But the...dangerous nature of my business there made that impossible this time."

"Speaking of which," Drakkal growled, "there's a whole lot I need to yell at you regarding that *business*, sedhi, so hurry this along."

Smirking, Arcanthus looked at Drakkal. "I will not be rushed in this, little pussycat. Wait your turn."

"Samantha, I'm sorry, but I don't think I'll be able to keep my promise to you."

Sam chuckled. "A promise is a promise. You can't break it."

At Arcanthus's urging, she removed the protective covering and peered into the container.

Her eyes rounded. "Is that... Oh my God, is that chocolate?"

There were several boxes of chocolate bars, both milk and

dark, boxes of fancily wrapped truffles, and hard candies neatly stacked within. The scent that struck her was strong enough to make her mouth water, and it was all the proof she needed that what she was seeing was real.

It'd been so, so long since she'd had chocolate.

Alongside the candy was an assortment of colorful boxes of tea. She grinned as she recalled the first time Arcanthus had tried the tea at her apartment. It hadn't been to his liking at all, but he'd clearly recognized its importance to her. She'd lost that precious supply when the Syndicate had attacked, along with her few other belongings.

She looked up at him. "You remembered."

"How could I forget, little flower?" Arcanthus purred. "It was not long after my first taste of tea that I had my first taste of your lips. Nothing will ever compare." He reached into the container and shifted some of the items, revealing more beneath them—several sketchbooks with thick, all-purpose paper and dozens of pencils, pens, markers, and paints in every color imaginable. "I know changing mediums can sometimes spark new inspiration."

"Arc... This is..."

"This isn't even all of it. But you will have to wait to see the rest."

Samantha slipped her arms around him from the side and pressed her body against his, hugging him tightly. "You didn't have to do this. All I wanted was you, home and safe. But thank you."

He shifted the container and wrapped his arm around her, resting his cheek atop her hair. "Being apart from you felt like a slow death, Samantha. These things don't make up for my absence, but I hope they show that I thought of you the entire time I was gone."

Sekk'thi chuckled. "It was a fun day of shopping."

Urgand snorted. "Yeah. Loads of fun. I'm still fucking sore."

"Was I wrong in assessing your strength, vorgal?" Arc asked. "If a few shopping bags was too much..."

"You bought enough stuff to open your own damned store, Arcanthus."

"That is an exaggeration," Sekk'thi said. "But only a slight one."

Samantha laughed. She could almost imagine Arcanthus walking down a busy sidewalk with Sekk'thi and Urgand in tow, the latter's arms laden with bags and stacks of boxes.

Arc huffed. "When did everyone get so dramatic?"

Drakkal snickered. "Yeah, I thought that was your job, sedhi."

"Come to think of it, Drakkal, I believe there's something in here for you." Arcanthus released Sam, and she stepped back as he carefully dug through the container, finally finding what he sought buried at the bottom.

Grinning, he produced a pink ball of yarn. "I understand this is very popular with cats back on Earth." He tossed the ball onto the floor. A string trailed behind it as it rolled to stop between Drakkal's feet. "Go on, give it a try."

Samantha covered her mouth to stifle more laughter as Drakkal stared flatly at Arc. She couldn't believe Arcanthus had actually done that.

Or maybe she could.

"Do you not like it, azhera?" Arcanthus asked, tilting his head and frowning. "It was purchased from the heart."

Nostrils flaring, Drakkal let out a long, slow breath. "I'm going to go find Thargen. See if he wants to smash something to tiny little pieces with me."

"But I only just got back, Drak."

Drakkal crouched and plucked the yarn from the floor.

When he straightened, he held it up and stared at it. "Urgand, you think someone would choke if this was shoved down their throat?"

Sam eased closer to Arcanthus and said in a soft voice, "Don't let him fool you. He missed you too."

"Oh, I know he did," Arc replied. Closing the container, he set it on the floor. Then he turned to face Samantha, dipping a hand into the pocket of his robe. "Now, if my dearest friend can curb his homicidal impulses for a few more moments..."

Arcanthus took a small box out of his pocket. "I know I've asked this before, Samantha, but I wanted to do it again the right way. The traditional terran way." Grasping the lid of the little box, Arcanthus sank to one knee and opened it. Upon the dark velvet lining the box was a ring bearing what looked to be a closed blossom wrought in white gold.

At least until he gave it a gentle tap.

As the blossom unfurled, he looked up into her eyes. "Samantha Dawn Wilder, my love, my mate, would you do me the honor of becoming my wife?"

Sam's breath caught, her heart skipped, and her eyes widened. Her hands reflexively rose to her mouth as she stared down at the ring. It was unlike anything she'd ever seen. The tiny, open petals were inlaid with gleaming rubies that perfectly matched the color Arcanthus so often wore, flawlessly rising from the intricate band as though they'd actually grown from it. At the center of the flower was a circular black opal, the flecks and swirls of color inside it shifting and flaring with the slightest movement under the light.

"For my flower," he said gently. "For my universe."

His universe. That black opal...it *did* look like the universe, with tiny galaxies swirling inside it.

Tears filled her eyes as they met his. She curled her fingers until her hands formed fists at her chin. "Oh Arc... My answer was yes then, and it's yes now. I've always been yours, and will always be yours, in every way possible."

The smile he offered in response was tender, affectionate, utterly adoring. He took her hand, and she extended her fingers, watching as he slipped on the ring.

"I never doubted it for a second, Samantha. Which is why I took the liberty of ensuring that, according to UTF records, you and I are legally married."

Samantha laughed and reached up to wipe away the tears falling from her eyes. "Of course you did."

Arcanthus reached for her and swept her into his arms as he stood. She giggled, threw her arms around his neck, and pressed a kiss to his cheek. His hold on her tightened. Without slowing, Arc strode toward the door leading into the compound.

"You really think you're getting away without having our friendly chat, sedhi?" Drakkal called from behind them.

"I've been away from my mate for far too long," Arcanthus replied, the corners of his mouth curling wickedly. "We can talk when I'm done making up for it."

VENGEFUL HEART   183

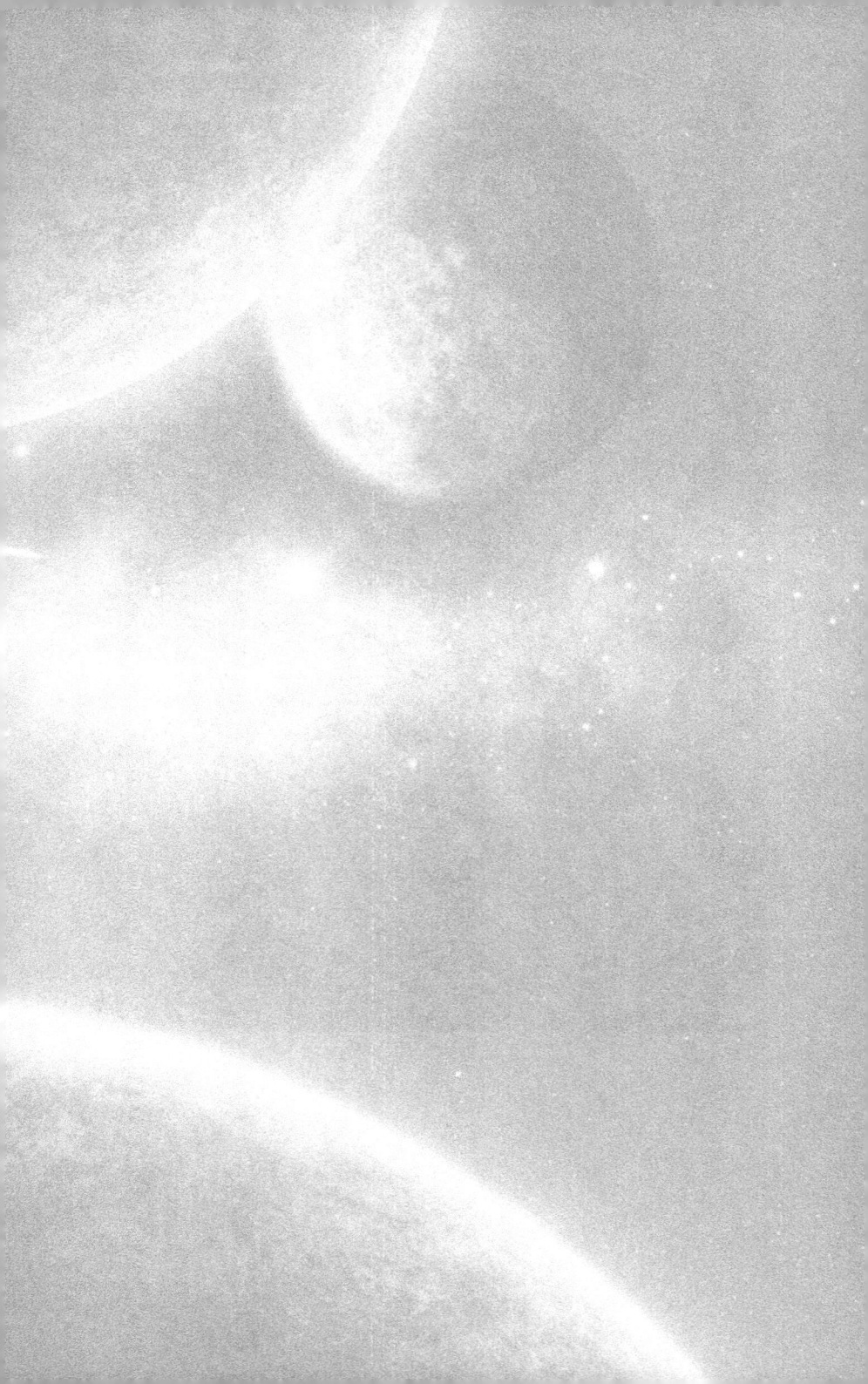

EPILOGUE

Arcanthus rolled his shoulders to adjust the lay of his tuxedo. His brief time on Earth hadn't made him any fonder of such restrictive clothing, but he didn't mind it today—because soon enough, he'd get to tear it off and toss it away to be forgotten.

"That really doesn't suit you," Drakkal said from behind him.

"You know, it's rather tiring to be the target of everyone else's insecurities," Arcanthus replied, smirking. "I'm sorry my ability to pull off any outfit threatens your self-esteem, Drakkal, but there's no changing perfection."

Drakkal snorted.

Frowning, Arc glanced over his shoulder at the azhera. "You're here for a purpose. Perhaps you should focus on it?"

Pressing his lips together, Drakkal stood a little straighter and clasped his hands in front of him, turning his gaze forward. "All right, sedhi. For Samantha, I'll pretend you don't look ridiculous. But only this one time."

"Thank you," Arcanthus muttered. "Truly, your compassion and generosity are boundless."

"Pretty sure you two are supposed to shut the fuck up until this thing starts," Thargen said from his seat.

"And you're one to talk?" Drakkal grumbled.

"No, I'm not supposed to talk either."

Sekk'thi silenced them with a hiss, and Arcanthus pinched the bridge of his nose, squeezing his eyes shut.

Drakkal cleared his throat with a growl. "All right, all right. We don't want to mess this up for Samantha."

"Yes. Please don't mess this up," Arc said. He opened his eyes to scan the room, feeling a flutter in his stomach. He couldn't be sure whether that feeling was anticipation, a touch of nervousness, or both. All this was foreign to him, and he had no idea if he was doing any of it correctly.

But he was comforted by his love for Samantha—and the understanding that she would love this regardless of the details he might have overlooked or misinterpreted. That couldn't stop him from wanting it perfect, but it was something.

No, not just something. It was...everything.

He and Drakkal stood on a low platform against the wall, directly opposite the room's entrance. A crimson carpet led from the door to the platform, with several chairs arranged on either side. Kiloq, Koroq, and Thargen sat to the left, Sekk'thi, Urgand, and Razi to the right, all dressed in clothing they wouldn't normally wear—*fancy* clothing.

A few hours of work had transformed the chamber from a bland space of concrete and cold lighting into a warm, intimate room. The decorations Arc had purchased on Earth had worked perfectly. The candles, ribbons, fake plants and flowers, and strands of starlike lights set a mood unlike anything that had ever existed here or in Arcanthus's prior compound. The table to the side of the door had been covered in an elaborate linen tablecloth and was now laden with gifts that were gathered around the centerpiece, a tiered cake created to the specifications of terran bakers. Though all this was only a fraction of the beauty his mate deserved to enjoy, it was undeniably beautiful.

And he'd only been able to put it together thanks to Abella's advice.

Arcanthus drew in a deep breath. He hadn't even seen Samantha today, owing to a terran tradition that forbid the bridegroom from seeing his bride prior to the ceremony on the day of their wedding. Even the dress she'd purchased for today was a mystery to him, as he'd rather reluctantly allowed her to go shopping for it without him, entrusting her safety to Drakkal and Sekk'thi.

His heart sped when the music began playing—an old terran song announcing the approach of the bride. He straightened and clasped his hands in front of him, squeezing tighter than he meant to; it was all he could do to prevent himself from racing toward the open door to meet her.

When Samantha appeared in the doorway, his heart stopped.

Instead of the customary white gown Abella had described, Samantha was swathed in crimson, creating a stark, tantalizing contrast between her dress and her pale skin. The bodice was adorned with intricate floral patterns, and its off-shoulder straps left her shoulders and collarbone bare. Sheer cloth hung from those straps, joining the voluminous train of her skirt.

Her brown hair was pulled up high in a mass of curls with tendrils hanging around a face that couldn't belong to anyone other than an enchantress.

And that enchantress was *his*.

Glittering red eyeshadow and black eyeliner framed her big brown eyes, which met and held his gaze. Her crimson lips spread into a wide smile.

"She is so fucking beautiful," Arcanthus breathed.

Samantha slowly walked toward him, holding a bouquet of blue, red, and violet flowers before her. Each step she took was one closer to Arcanthus, to their destiny, to the life they'd chosen to share, and each of those steps only intensified her happiness. Joy radiated from her eyes and her smile, neither of which had ever been so bright as they were now.

The tangled, difficult paths their lives had followed, the struggles they'd endured, the pain, loss, and fear, had led them here, to this moment. Had led them to each other.

Arcanthus knew Samantha's past still haunted her, he knew those wounds hadn't fully healed, but the monster who'd inflicted them was dead. Arc would do everything in his power to abolish the shadow James had cast over Sam, and he would never let darkness fall over her again.

When Samantha stepped onto the little platform and turned to face Arcanthus, his whole body tensed; he yearned to grab her right then and kiss her until all those old scars had faded forever.

As he looked into her eyes, serenity settled over him, spawned by the knowledge that this moment was exactly as it was meant to be. He was here, with her, about to be joined in the tradition of her people—already joined in every other way that mattered. This was right. This was real.

She set her bouquet on the floor beside her. Arcanthus held out his hands, and she took them, beaming up at him with a wide smile.

Drakkal drew in a deep breath and released it with just a hint of a grunt. "I'm sure you both want to keep this short, and I don't really know what I'm doing, but..." He withdrew a piece of paper from his pocket and unfolded it, staring down at the hastily scrawled words. "All of us come from different galaxies. From different cultures. We've all been through some shit."

"More like a lot of shit," Kiloq said.

Koroq elbowed his brother. "Shut up."

Samantha pressed her lips together, stifling a laugh.

"And though none of us can ever know exactly what the others experienced"—Drakkal's eyes flicked to Arcanthus—"even when we were together for a lot of it, we've all found common ground. We've found friendship. We've found family. And it's all right here, in this room. So, we're here now, getting paid overtime, to join these two in the sacred bond of marriage."

Arcanthus arched a brow. "Overtime, azhera?"

"*Kraasz ka'val*, sedhi, lighten up. It's a joke." Drakkal lifted his gaze to the onlookers and shook his head. "Anyway, uh... Right. Marriage. Not all of us are familiar with it, but we all know of something similar. Mates. Lifebonds. Whatever we call it, all of us recognize love as a real thing. Sometimes, that means pain and loss. But a couple like Arcanthus and Samantha prove that the good will always outshine the bad. That even arrogant, self-absorbed pricks like this sedhi are capable of finding love and reciprocating."

"Even at my own wedding," Arcanthus muttered.

"You really want it any different?" Drakkal asked.

Samantha chuckled. Giving Arc's fingers a squeeze, she leaned closer and whispered. "I don't think you're any of those things." She paused. "Well, maybe a little arrogant, but I love you anyway."

Drakkal cleared his throat. "We all do. You've given all of us a place and a purpose, Arc. And I can speak for everyone when I say we're honored to be part of this. Samantha has brought new life to this place, and more importantly, she's brought new life to you. She's reminded us that there's plenty of things in the universe to cherish and protect. And we really appreciate that we don't lose our credits to *only* Razi anymore."

The others—minus Razi—gave a little cheer from their seats.

"All right." Drakkal shifted the paper in his big fingers. "So, hopefully I got this right. Arcanthus, do you take Samantha Dawn Wilder as your wife to care for, love, and protect no matter what kind of shit you're both going through?"

Arcanthus stared deep into his mate's beautiful brown eyes. "Always and forever."

"Samantha Dawn Wilder, do you take Arcanthus as your husband to care for, love, and protect no matter what kind of shit he is going through?"

Eyes misting with tears, Samantha held his gaze as she said, "I do. In every way I can."

"Then by my authority as head of security and everyone's second fucking mother, I pronounce you husband and wife. Now you can kiss. But keep your damned clothes on, all right?"

Arcanthus tugged his *wife* against him. She came eagerly, throwing her arms around his neck. Banding his arms around her, he palmed her ass, cupped the back of her head, and slanted his mouth over hers as he leaned her back in a dip. Her soft mouth yielded to his kiss. He drank in her sweetness, savored her warmth, relished her lovely scent.

Wife.

Mate.

Lover.

Samantha was all that and so much more. She was his heart, his soul.

His everything.

Heat coalesced within him, and his chest constricted with a flood of emotion. It didn't seem possible to feel so much, so strongly, all at once, but there it was—and by far the strongest of those emotions was his love for the female in his arms.

He broke the contact between their lips only to press a gentle kiss to the tip of her nose, followed by another on her forehead, and finally one atop her hair. Looking down into her eyes, he smiled. "I love you, my flower, and I will always fight for you. From one side of the universe to the other."

AUTHOR'S NOTE

It always bothered me that Samantha's ex never received punishment for what he did to her, that he just got away with it, and it's something I've thought about from time to time. So when inspiration hit, we knew we had to give Sam justice...and who better to deliver it than her mate, Arcanthus?

We hope you guys enjoyed this addition to the Infinite City series. It was fun to revisit older characters and allow them more time to interact with one another.

And if you'd like to read a little more about Urgand and Sekk'thi...turn the page! We have some bonus content for you. :D See what these two were up to while Arcanthus was taking care of business.

URGENT & SEKK'THIU

BONUS CONTENT

CHAPTER 1

"Can't fucking believe he did this again," Urgand snarled as he stared down at the paper in his hand. "What the fuck is wrong with him?"

For the twentieth time, he reread the note.

To My Favorite Employee (and also the vorgal),

Early meeting for me this morning. Feel free to take the day for yourselves. But please ensure that any expenses incurred are settled via your personal accounts and not *with company funds.*

Warmest Regards,
The Best Boss You'll Ever Have

Urgand growled. How was he always surprised by the sedhi's behavior, even after years of living and working with him? This sort of thing wasn't new.

Sekk'thi emerged from the bedroom, wearing one of those ilthurii dresses made from blue and purple fabric. The loose ends of the cloth dangled around her, creating a layer effect that rippled and flowed with her movements.

And Urgand couldn't help but notice the way it complemented her body. It accentuated the grace of her lithe limbs and tail, brought out the brilliant green of her scales, and showed off her lean but powerful muscles.

She tilted her head and blinked as she drew near. "You are staring, vorgal."

His nostrils flared with a heavy breath. "I am."

Halting a few meters away from him, she spread her arms and glanced down at herself. "Do I look strange?"

Urgand shook his head. "You look...fucking hot."

Her lips twitched up in an uncharacteristically uncertain smile. "That is kind of you to say, but you do not need to lie."

"Not lying, Sekk'thi."

She narrowed her eyes as she regarded him, though her expression soon softened. "I am unused to such clothing. Just like Arcanthus with his suits."

Urgand smiled. "Yeah, but at least you don't whine about it."

Sekk'thi laughed, and her tail swung a little faster. "Were you talking to yourself?"

He arched a brow. "Talking to you, obviously."

She shook her head and stepped closer. "A few moments ago. Before I joined you."

The heat in Urgand's core spread to his cheeks. He didn't understand his own reaction; what was there to be embarrassed about? He and Sekk'thi were friends. They'd fought together, bled together, drank and laughed together. By Vorga's flaming skull, she'd even seem him bare-assed once or twice thanks to the cren brothers' pranks.

He grunted and shrugged. "Guess it was half to myself, half

to Arc. But he's not around to hear it, so I'm left looking like a damned fool."

"He is not here?"

Sighing, Urgand handed her the note.

"I did not know people still wrote by hand on paper," she said, turning the sheet as she studied it. "We wrote by hand in the pens, but it always in the dirt or on stone. Paper would have been a welcome thing."

Urgand frowned and gritted his teeth. His gut tightened, twisting on itself, and echoes of something he'd not felt in a long, long time rippled through him—Rage.

Though Sekk'thi rarely spoke of her past, everyone on the crew knew the story, if only in its simplest version. She'd been born as something even less than a slave, raised in pens alongside her brethren as food. That she'd eventually escaped the ordeal was incredible, but it didn't make Urgand any less angry about what she'd suffered, and that anger had only intensified as he'd come to know her better over the years.

And he didn't know what to say about it. He only knew that she didn't seem to need his words, didn't seem to need his anger, leaving him to hope that his friendship, his presence, was enough.

Sekk'thi read the note and hummed thoughtfully. "So, he did it again."

"He did. Must've left before the sun even came up."

She nodded, placed the note on the table, and faced the window. The city was alive, its metal and glass gleaming in the morning light in a way almost reminiscent of Arthos's surface.

"Should we attempt to track him?" she asked. "He must have left some trail, however faint."

Rage simmered in Urgand's heart as he looked upon her. Contemplative, compassionate, easygoing, selfless, strong;

Sekk'thi was all that and more. And she'd been denied so much in her life. She'd endured such hardship.

"No. He can take care of himself, and we're off today," Urgand replied. "Fuck him."

"Fuck him?"

"Not literally."

Sekk'thi blinked. "I know that, Urgand."

He grunted and snatched up the note. "He ran off alone again and told us we're not working today. All I'm saying is that we should take advantage of it."

Her eyes brightened. "So we can do more shopping?"

Urgand cringed, barely suppressing a shudder. "Only if you want to torture me."

She cocked her head, and her eyes dipped, raking over his body. "Hmm."

He chuckled, and that heat worked its way back down into his lower belly, sending a pulse straight to his groin. It took all his willpower not to growl in response.

Somehow, he managed a natural tone when he said, "We had a good time last night, right?"

Again, her tail quickened, and she nodded. "I enjoyed the hamburgers. And the drinks afterward."

"Because I was with you, right?"

She displayed a bit more of her teeth. "I would have enjoyed them alone also. They tasted good." Lowering her head, she closed the distance between herself and Urgand and looked up into his eyes. "But I enjoyed the company most of all."

His heart thumped against his ribs, and his lips stretched into a wide grin. With Sekk'thi this close, her scent was stronger than any other—sun and spice, a hint of sand and exotic flowers.

"We should go out today. Take advantage of the free time," he said.

"It is early for hamburgers and alcohol, Urgand."

He laughed. "Not by vorgal standards. But that's not what I mean, anyway."

"What then?"

His mind again went back to what he knew of her past, to all the experiences she'd never had, all the things she'd never done or seen. To a comment she'd made while she, Urgand, and Arc had been descending from orbit in the shuttle.

"Well...it's a surprise," he said. "You trust me?"

A flicker of color—deep purple—coursed across the paler scales of her throat, there and gone in an instant. The light in her violet eyes grew brighter than ever. "I do."

Urgand's grin eased. He crumpled the paper and tossed it atop the table. "Good. Then come with me."

CHAPTER 2

After riding on a train car packed near to bursting with passengers, Urgand was grateful for the brine-kissed breeze that flowed around him as he and Sekk'thi climbed the stairs to the boardwalk. He drew in a deep breath, ignoring all the other scents to focus on that of the sea.

As she reached the top of the steps, Sekk'thi gasped, and her pace faltered. She continued forward almost robotically, her gaze fixed on the sight beyond the boardwalk railing. None of the diverse people all around, none of the colorful shops, booths, and attractions, none of the foreign smells or cries of excitement could draw her attention away from the gray-blue waters stretching out ahead.

Urgand walked alongside her, acting as a living barrier between the entranced ilthurii and the other pedestrians. She stopped only when the railing blocked her way, absently placing her hands atop it.

"Urgand," she rasped, her eyes shifting from side to side as she beheld the ocean.

Though there was so much to see, he couldn't look away

from her. Sekk'thi's kind was known for having relatively unexpressive faces, but surely that reputation had been attributed to them by people who were entirely unobservant; her face brimmed with emotions, her eyes shone with wonder and joy.

He smiled. "Hmm?"

"It is..." Sekk'thi shook her head, jaws parting, and leaned back. "It is...so big. It goes on forever."

Bracing an elbow on the railing, he finally forced himself to look seaward. People were all over the beach, lounging on chairs or atop blankets and towels spread on the pale sand, walking along the shoreline, playing in the surf.

And they were all so tiny compared to the ocean, which ran right up to the blue sky on the distant horizon. Rolling waves lapped at the sand, foaming white as they crested.

Urgand had seen beaches on half a dozen worlds. He'd walked on the sand with sea spray in his face and waves crashing nearby, had stood on the edge of a cliff with wind raging around him and dark, expansive waters churning below. He'd waded in calm, clear ocean waters, through which he'd seen every speck of sand, every clump of alien vegetation, every shell, every stone. He had all those memories...

But this beach, this ocean, was the first he'd ever truly beheld, and it was thanks to Sekk'thi. Through her eyes, he could see the beauty and majesty. He could experience the wonder.

"You want to go down there?" he asked.

Her gaze lingered on the water before she turned her head to look along the boardwalk.

"Not yet," she said, releasing the railing. "Let us see all this, first."

Urgand pushed himself upright and gestured her onward. "Anything you'd like, Sekk'thi."

Side-by-side, they ventured forth. Rides and games abound,

though nothing was quite so eye-catching as the towering, railed structures the terrans called roller coasters. As the pair stood at the base of one such ride, which was constructed of huge steel struts and beams, Sekk'thi wondered aloud what the appeal was of such things.

After one of the hanging cars, filled with screaming passengers, sped by overhead, Urgand offered his best guess. "All about the thrill. The perception of danger, the rush of speed, the sense that you have no control. All you can do is sit back and enjoy the ride. Maybe for terrans, it's a way to feel more alive for a couple minutes. It's like that for a lot of people."

She regarded him with her head cocked. "And for you?"

He studied the rails, noting all the empty air beneath them, and shrugged. "Only one way to find out."

They met each other's gazes, grinned, and hurried to join the queue.

Fifteen minutes later, they were strapped into their seats with rigid, over the shoulder harnesses secured and legs dangling. Sekk'thi's pupils had expanded, shrinking the violet of her eyes.

"Nervous?" he asked.

"Yes. But I think it is in a good way," she replied.

The car started, entering an incline. With the warm breeze, the unbroken view of the ocean, beach, and boardwalk, and the blue sky with its soft white clouds overhead, the ride was almost relaxing.

Beside him, Sekk'thi sat with her feet swinging and her tail tucked over her lap.

Might have to thank Arc for being an asshole.

Because had Arcanthus not run off again, Urgand wouldn't have been here with Sekk'thi right now, making the most unexpected, thrilling memories.

The car reached the apex of the incline, and for an instant, everything slowed down. Urgand glanced at Sekk'thi. Her eyes were rounded, her sharp teeth bared, and her hands were clenched on the handles attached to the harness.

Urgand grinned. He'd ridden more dropships down from orbit than he could count, and the experienced soldiers had always enjoyed seeing the fresh recruits react to their first drop. This wasn't much different.

He faced forward.

The car turned down—and plunged straight toward the ground.

Urgand's balls leapt up into his guts, which themselves jumped into his throat. He'd never had to feel the wind in his hair during a drop, had never had to stare directly at the ground, which was approaching so quickly.

Sekk'thi let out a delighted laugh.

Urgand laughed too, hoping it didn't sound as nervous as it felt.

Though he didn't voice it, he was overcome by gratitude when he and Sekk'thi disembarked the ride and set their feet on solid ground. His insides felt like they'd been thrashed around by all the drops, twists, and flips.

"That was fun," Sekk'thi said, bouncing on her feet.

Urgand offered the most honest response he could muster. "Thargen would've loved it."

Sekk'thi grasped his wrist and tugged him along. "Come, Urgand. There are more rides I would like to try."

He chuckled to himself. "Anything you like, Sekk'thi. Anything."

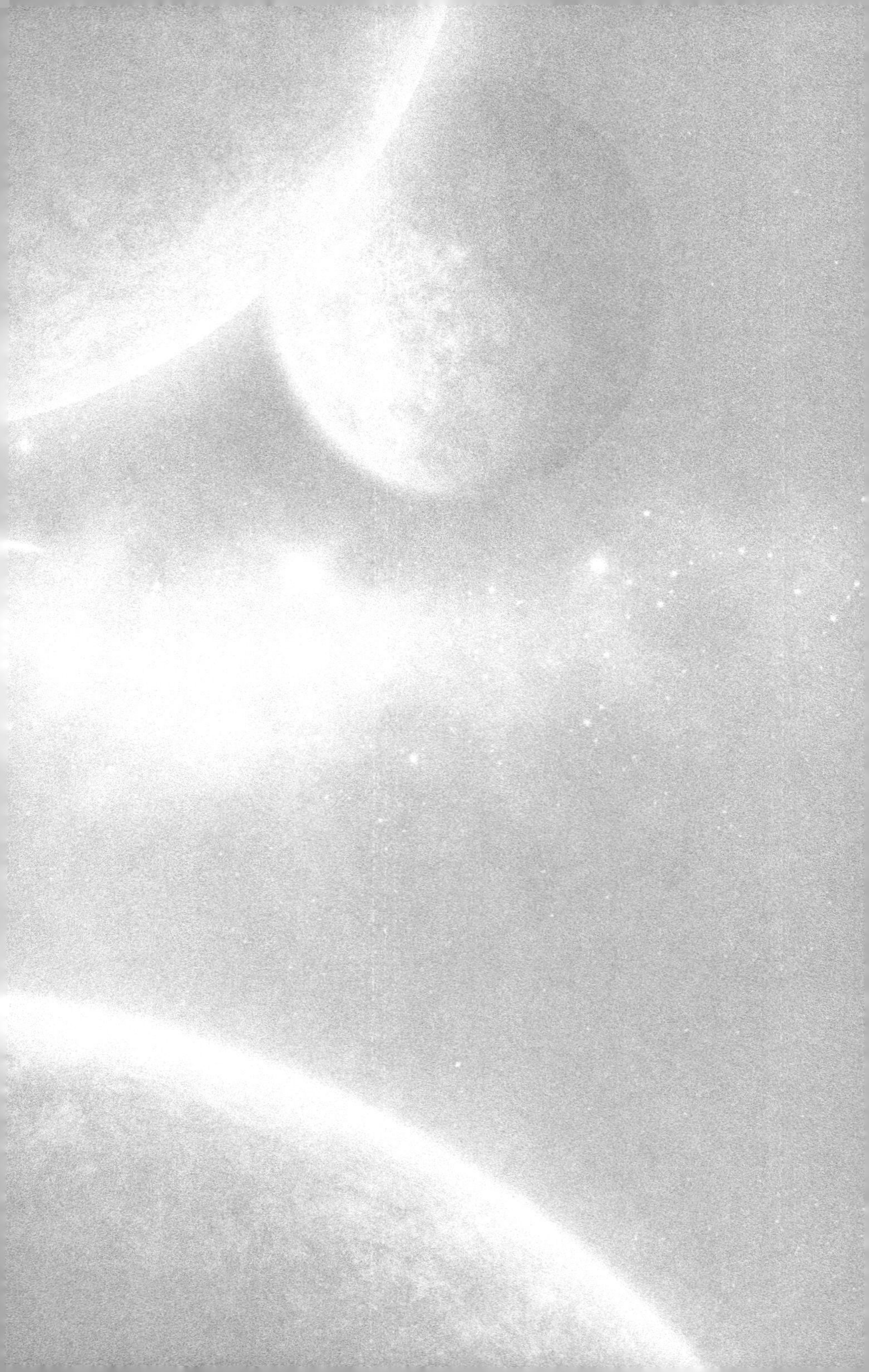

CHAPTER 3

"Going to take a piss," Urgand said.

Sekk'thi nodded, flashing a toothy smile. She had her prize from one of the games tucked precariously beneath one arm—a massive plush monstrosity with long, floppy ears, pink and purple fur, and disturbingly blank black eyes. "I will wait here. Unless...you need help?"

Something shifted in that smile, and it speared Urgand's lower belly with heat.

"Think I can manage."

"Hmm..." She shifted the plush toy to hold it in both arms at her front and cocked her head. "Very well, Urgand."

"Back in a minute." He turned and followed the blue signs that he believed pointed toward the lavatories, unable to shake the suspicion that he'd just missed an opportunity.

When the fuck did I become so timid?

He grunted as he descended a set of steps leading into a narrow walkway. Timid wasn't the right word. Uncertain fit much better, perhaps even with a dash of *cautious*. The way he'd been trained, the things he'd experienced...

Urgand had spoken to Thargen about it a few times over the years. The lingering effects of their time in the Vanguard weren't all the same, but they had enough in common to understand one another. Where Thargen struggled to control his Rage—and himself—Urgand struggled to tap into it at all. Flying into a fury didn't help a medic stabilize a wounded soldier. While everyone else in the Vanguard had been trained and drugged to enhance their Rage, the medics and officers had been conditioned to suppress it.

And what the fuck was a vorgal without his Rage?

Shoving those thoughts aside, he glanced up. The blue signs directed him into an intersecting alley; he let out a heavy breath and turned the corner.

Having a good day. A really fucking good day. Why am I trying to screw it up by thinking about this shit? Why—

"The fuck?" someone asked.

Urgand halted and glanced up. A group of people were gathered ahead—a female azhera, a male borian, and three male terrans, all wearing clothing with crimson accents. One of the terrans was holding out a vial of electric blue liquid to another, but they were all staring at Urgand.

"Lavatory down this way?" Urgand asked.

All five of the crimson-clad people scowled.

"Wrong alley, vorgal," the borian said. He stood a head taller than his companions, with broad shoulders and powerful arms. The tip of one of his long, pointed ears was missing.

The terran slipped the vial into his pocket. "Wrong time, too."

Urgand's heart quickened, and he barely kept a smile off his face. Whatever his issues, he always enjoyed a good fight—but a fight was exactly what he was supposed to avoid here on Earth. He lifted his hands, displaying his palms. "Didn't see anything."

"Bullshit," another terran snapped.

"I just need to take a piss."

"You will, vorgal, long before this is done," the azhera said as she stepped forward.

These thugs were young and eager, undoubtedly emboldened by their number advantage. That they had something to prove was evident in their eyes; Urgand had seen it all too often in Arthos's criminal underworld. And even if the thought of running didn't make him bristle inside, he wasn't likely to outrun the azhera.

Still, fleeing and calling for help would've been the sensible thing...

"Fuck," Urgand muttered, lowering his hands. "You're determined to get me in trouble with my boss, aren't you?"

"Your boss is going to have to scrape what's left of you off the concrete," the third terran said, slipping metal knuckles over his fingers.

Sighing, Urgand assumed a fighting stance. "Whenever you all regain consciousness, remember to tell the rest of your little gang that you were outnumbered three to one. I wouldn't want your reputations ruined."

"Fuck you," one of them spat; Urgand couldn't tell who, and it didn't matter, because those words were the spark that ignited the fight.

Three of them rushed at him, with the azhera as their spearhead. Urgand growled and batted aside their wild attacks, forcing them to bump and stumble into one another in the limited space of the alleyway. His fist darted out in a counterattack, catching a terran on the jaw and sending the male reeling, but another of the terrans forced his way forward to fill the gap.

Urgand didn't have a single conscious thought during the ensuing flurry of blows. Everything was instinct and muscle memory as he blocked and evaded, afforded no opportunities to retaliate.

"Drop his ass already!" someone called.

The azhera's claws sliced through the air a centimeter from Urgand's nose. He caught hold of her arm and swung her hard, slamming her face-first into the wall. One of the terran's fists struck his ribs, and pain blossomed across his side. He snarled and hammered his elbow into the back of the azhera's head. She grunted and sagged, and he released his hold.

The borian rushed forward with a heavy kick that caught Urgand in the chest. The air exploded from Urgand's lungs, and he slid back, but he managed to seize hold of the borian's long leg, dragging his foe along with him.

Overextended, the borian flailed his arms to regain control. Urgand tugged hard on the leg, forcing the borian down into a split. His knee was already rising to meet the borian's chin.

Even as that attack connected and snapped the borian's head back, two more blows struck Urgand—the metal knuckles on one of the terrans' fists hit his gut, and the boot of another terran hit his face.

Urgand staggered backward, keeping himself upright only by slapping a hand against the alley wall. He wiped his mouth; his hand came away bloodied. Fire flared in his chest, totally separate from the burn of having had his lungs forcibly emptied. "Berrok's bare ass, you're going to pay for that one."

Groaning, the azhera dragged herself onto her feet, and the borian was struggling to roll over onto his hands and knees. The terrans were all up, including one with a bloody nose, who drew a tristeel knife from his belt. The third terran extended a collapsible shock baton.

"Only one person's going to fucking pay, vorgal," the terran with the broken nose snarled.

"This does not seem fair," Sekk'thi said from behind Urgand.

Urgand couldn't stop a grin from stretching across his lips, the expression bringing with it a sharp pain as it widened split on his lower lip. That sting was exhilarating.

"Who the fuck is this scaly bitch?" demanded the borian as he finally stood up, shaking his head hard.

The heat within Urgand intensified a hundredfold, and crimson stained the edges of his vision. He clenched his fists. The tendons stood out starkly on the backs of his hands, which trembled with building fury.

Sekk'thi stepped up beside Urgand, just visible in his peripheral vision. She said, "I am with you."

Those words drove him to action.

The battle became a chaotic blur in which time had no meaning. Urgand was aware only of his blows landing on his enemies, and of Sekk'thi, so controlled and graceful, yet so powerful, moving beside him, anticipating his movements like she could read his mind. He was aware of...rightness, though everything about this situation should've been wrong.

The gang made a hasty, stumbling retreat, all but carrying the dazed borian, whose head lolled with every step.

Raw, bestial instinct urged Urgand to give chase and end this now, to ensure that his enemies never came back. That instinct pulsed with Rage. He clenched his fists and resisted, knowing nothing good would come of furthering this conflict.

His breaths were ragged, his racing heartbeat was like the pounding of war drums, and his knuckles were throbbing and bloodied, but he shook off his Rage as quickly as it had come on. Turning toward Sekk'thi, he looked her over. "You hurt?"

Strips of fabric dangled from her dress, some tattered and torn, some attached by single threads.

She glanced down at herself and let out a hiss. "I am

unharmed, but I cannot say the same for my clothing." Working quickly, she used her claws to slice threads and cut away loose cloth. The result was a bit more revealing than before, but Urgand wouldn't have been able to tell the dress had been damaged to begin with.

"Better," she said, offering him that ilthurii smile as she wadded up the fabric and threading. That smile fell as she stepped closer. "What of you, Urgand? You are bleeding."

He reached up to wipe his lip again, only to stop when he caught sight of his hands. "I've been through a fuck of a lot worse. Most painful part is going to be when my lip splits open again, because it always does. Just need to take a minute to clean up."

She pointed down the alley. "I believe the lavatories are just there. I will take a moment to clean up also."

Urgand nodded, and they walked to the lavatories together, splitting to enter separate rooms. After a good wash-up—followed by him finally emptying his bladder and washing up again—he rejoined Sekk'thi outside.

Her prize was tucked under her arm again. He would always remember the light that had been in her eyes when she'd won it after knocking over what must've been dozens of cans at a carnival booth. "It may be best for us to return to the hotel."

"You're right. They're not going to go to law enforcement, but they'll probably be back with some friends sooner or later." Sighing, he glanced skyward. The clouds had taken on a red-orange tint as the day approached its end. "But there's one more thing we still need to do."

"What is that?"

He offered her his hand. "Come on. I'll show you."

Urgand led her back up to the boardwalk and across it, taking another set of steps down toward the beach.

She halted on the final step, pulling her hand back. Brow furrowed, Urgand glanced at her.

"Would you hold this?" She held out the plush, and when he took it, she braced a hand on the railing and bent down. "So many people speak of this sensation. I want to experience it myself."

Urgand watched as she removed her sandals from her clawed feet, hooking them over her fingers, and smiled. Hopping to keep his balance, he lifted a foot and untied his boot, managing to tug it off without falling—but only barely.

Sekk'thi laughed and took the plush back from him. Her smile didn't fade as he removed his other boot.

When he was done, she stepped down onto the sand. Her feet sank into it, and some of it came through her clawed toes, making her laugh again. Urgand moved into place beside her. Had he ever done this since he was young? When was the last time he'd been on a beach outside of a combat zone?

"Let's go," he said, offering his arm.

She slipped her arm through his, and they walked toward the water. The sun was setting in the distance, its light shimmering on the rolling waves, making them sparkle and glow. The red, orange, and yellow in the sky faded to blue and purple on the opposite horizon. Sea breeze flowed through Urgand's hair and caressed his skin, but it wasn't a fraction as enticing as the feel of Sekk'thi's warm scales against his skin.

They stopped where the wet sand was more solid underfoot and stood, side by side, as the surf swept over their feet and ankles, its chill a welcome contrast to the warmth of the sun.

Sekk'thi was silent, her eyes scanning the water, sky, and beach, taking in everything with the same wonder she'd displayed upon their arrival that morning. Her emerald scales shimmered in the sunset. All the beauty struck Urgand anew, reflected and magnified through her. Though the aches and pains from the recent fight didn't go away, he could ignore them during these moments.

It wasn't often that someone displayed such pure, unabashed happiness, and he wouldn't miss it for anything.

She brushed her swaying tail across the backs of his legs, sending a thrill up his spine. "The way the water moves, the way the light plays upon it, the size, it is all…"

"Beautiful. It's beautiful," he said. "So are you."

Slowly, she pried her gaze from the sea, her expression softening as her eyes met his. Faint purple appeared on her throat. "You do not mean such things."

With a disbelieving chuckle, Urgand shook his head. "All that you've overcome, all you've survived, and you still can't see yourself?" He released her arm, turned to face her fully, and cradled the side of her face with his hand. "Damn it, Sekk'thi, you *are* beautiful. You fucking shine."

She made a quiet sound, somewhere between a purr and a hum, and leaned into his touch. "When I am with you."

"No, Sekk'thi. All the fucking time." He leaned closer, and she lifted her nose, exposing her neck—which was a deeper purple than ever. Something in her scent had changed, had sweetened and become even more alluring, and he knew that this was an invitation. Urgand pressed his lips to the soft scales of her throat.

Sekk'thi purred again, dropping her sandals to reach around and cup the back of his head as he caressed her neck with his mouth and grazed her with his tusks.

"Now we should return to the hotel," she said.

Urgand lifted his head, frowning. "Why's that?"

A ravenous, playful light flared in her violet eyes, and her fingers flexed, teasing his flesh with her claws. She pressed her forehead to his and curled her tail around his back, pulling him close. "Because there is an audience here, vorgal."

ALSO BY TIFFANY ROBERTS

THE INFINITE CITY

Entwined Fates

Silent Lucidity

Shielded Heart

Vengeful Heart

Untamed Hunger

Savage Desire

Tethered Souls

THE KRAKEN

Treasure of the Abyss

Jewel of the Sea

Hunter of the Tide

Heart of the Deep

Rising from the Depths

Fallen from the Stars

Lover from the Waves

THE SPIDER'S MATE TRILOGY

Ensnared

Enthralled

Bound

THE VRIX
The Weaver
The Delver
The Hunter

THE CURSED ONES
His Darkest Craving

His Darkest Desire

ALIENS AMONG US
Taken by the Alien Next Door

Stalked by the Alien Assassin

Claimed by the Alien Bodyguard

STANDALONE TITLES
Claimed by an Alien Warrior

Dustwalker

Escaping Wonderland

Yearning For Her

The Warlock's Kiss

Ice Bound: Short Story

ISLE OF THE FORGOTTEN
Make Me Burn

Make Me Hunger

Make Me Whole

Make Me Yours

VALOS OF SONHADRA COLLABORATION

Tiffany Roberts - Undying

Tiffany Roberts - Unleashed

VENYS NEEDS MEN COLLABORATION

Tiffany Roberts - To Tame a Dragon

Tiffany Roberts – To Love a Dragon

ABOUT THE AUTHOR

Tiffany Roberts is the pseudonym for Tiffany and Robert Freund, a husband and wife writing duo. The two have always shared a passion for reading and writing, and it was their dream to combine their mighty powers to create the sorts of books they want to read. They write character driven sci-fi and fantasy romance, creating happily-ever-afters for the alien and unknown.

**Sign up for our Newsletter!
Check out our social media sites and more!
http://www.authortiffanyroberts.com**